Take a Chance on Me

A MISTY RIVER ROMANCE NOVELLA

Becky Wade

My very sincere thanks to the following people, who all gave of their time to assist me with the creation of this novella: Charlene Patterson, Group Captain Willy Hackett, Debb Hackett, Joy Tiffany, Crissy Loughridge, Shelli Littleton, and Natalie Walters.

I'm truly grateful to each of you!

Chapter One

The hospital's electronic doors whooshed open as Penelope Quinn rushed toward the emergency room.

She'd been at Cork & Knife, having dinner with friends in downtown Misty River, when she'd received a terrifying call from her older brother, Theo. Breaking every speed limit between the restaurant and the hospital, she'd made it here in just twelve minutes.

Immediately upon reaching the ER's waiting room, she spotted Theo. Her tall sibling stood like a tree in a field of linoleum and chairs. He'd married his sweet-natured blond wife, Aubrey, three years ago. And ten days ago, Aubrey had given birth to their first child. A snowy white burp cloth rested over his shoulder and he held his new baby, Madeline, against it as he turned toward Penelope. "I'm so glad you're here."

"Tell me more about what happened."

"One of Aubrey's legs swelled up and then she started having chest pain. She was dizzy, coughing, struggling to breathe. I called 911. As soon as the ambulance took her, Madeline and I got in the car to come here. That's when I called you." Worry had turned his even features pale and bleak. His hand appeared rigid against Madeline's tiny, rounded back.

"Did they tell you what caused her symptoms?"

"They think a blood clot formed in her leg and traveled to her lungs. It's called a pulmonary embolism, and, apparently, a woman's at greater risk for it after delivering a baby."

Penelope flinched. A blood clot had killed Aubrey's dad a few years ago. If something happened to Aubrey . . .

Nothing could happen to Aubrey. She was a brand-new mother and the cool, quiet breeze of their passionate, emotional family. The only outcome of this emergency: Aubrey recovering and returning home to be a mother to Madeline, wife to Theo, website designer to her employer. *That's it. That's what must happen.*

"I need to go back and check on her," Theo said. "But I don't want to expose Madeline to even more germs than I am already."

"Exactly. I'll take over with Madeline so you can focus on Aubrey."

"I forgot to bring her diaper bag. I'm sorry. She's sleeping now but I'm sure she'll be hungry soon."

"Don't worry about a thing." Without Aubrey to calm this terrifying situation, it was up to her and her brother to keep it together. "I've got this." It was what people said to pump themselves up when they suspected, like Penelope suspected now, that they *did not* have this. "I'll drive Madeline back to your house and get her situated."

"Take my car. It has the base for the baby seat." He fished his keys from his pocket and handed them, and then his daughter, to her.

Penelope carefully settled her niece's warm weight against her.

"Oh, and I also called . . ." His attention latched onto a point behind her. "Good. Here he is now."

"Who?"

"Eli. I called him after I called you."

Nooooo. That one word magnified and lessened in volume within her skull like a tornado siren. The very last person she wanted to deal with at present was her brother's friend, fighter pilot Eli Price. He'd been deployed to Syria for five months.

Then the Air Force had given him a month off, which he'd spent with family in his home state of Montana. No one had told her he'd returned to Georgia.

It would have been better for her peace of mind had he set himself up with a home, a lawn, a dog, and citizenship overseas.

She braced herself and slowly swiveled to look. A smattering of people inhabited the waiting room. All the female heads in the place, even the ailing ones, were also tracking Eli's progress.

He'd dressed his lean six-foot frame in a simple black polo shirt and jeans. He was thirty years old and, already, hard proficiency marked his forehead, the set of his eyebrows, and the positioning of his straight nose. His jawline formed a wide, very determined V. Yet, his deep-set brown eyes and his lips were soft in the most irresistible way. His dark blond hair, which he kept as long as Air Force regulations allowed, looked as if it would soon be in need of a trim. Charmingly so.

His intelligent gaze took her measure. "Penelope."

"Eli." She pretended interest in smoothing the burp cloth beneath Madeline's face.

The two men exchanged a brief, masculine hug and stepped apart. "Thanks for coming," Theo said.

"I'm glad you called."

"I'm not sure what's going on or how long Aubrey will be here." Theo motioned between himself and Penelope. "Our mom and dad and Aubrey's mom were all here for Madeline's birth and for several days afterward. But our folks are back in Boston and Aubrey's mom is back in Arizona. I figured Penelope might need a hand with Madeline."

"Right. I'm happy to help."

God love you, my very excellent brother. But I do not need the help of this particular man when caring for Madeline.

"I was also hoping you could coach my basket-ball team for me," Theo said to Eli. "One of Aubrey's friends talked me into coaching her son's second grade team. We have a game tomorrow and my assistant coach isn't capable of taking the lead."

"Sure."

"Thanks. I'll text more information about that to you when I have time." He threw a glance toward the ER. Hesitated. "I should check on Aubrey. Are you guys set? Need anything else?"

"Yes, we're set and no, we don't need anything else," Penelope assured him. "I'll take fantastic care of Madeline. Just let me know when you have more information about Aubrey, okay?"

"'Kay." He gave her a side-armed hug, kissed Madeline on the head, then walked through swinging metal doors.

Ever since Theo had mentioned germs, Penelope had been wishing she could cover her niece's face with a gas mask. "How about we relocate to fresh air?"

"All right. Do you want me to take her?"

"No, thank you." She gestured with her chin toward Madeline's baby seat, sitting on a nearby chair. He grasped it and she led the way from the building.

On this second-to-last day of June, the hours of daylight per day had recently hit their annual peak. Bronze sun still graced the North Georgia mountains at this hour of the evening. It dappled her shoulders as she stopped several yards from the entrance, beneath a tree. It slanted across Eli's eyelashes as he came to a halt facing her.

Her senses struggled to adjust to the reality of him after six months of distance. He was, to her ever-loving irritation, *more appealing* than she'd remembered. His eyes more perceptive, his manner more assured.

Should she just bluntly state that she didn't

want or need his help—

"I missed you," he said.

The statement surprised her to such a degree, was so, so . . . *absurd*, that she released a gasp of laughter. "No, you didn't."

"Yes, I did."

"No."

"I think I know what I felt while I was gone better than you do," he said good-naturedly. "I missed you."

"Fine." But her tone communicated *that's ridiculous*.

"It's really good to see you." The affection in his expression gave weight and breadth to the statement.

She could not, however, let the affection she saw there soften *her*. "When did you get back?"

"Three days ago."

"Welcome," she said stiffly. She did not say *welcome home* because Misty River was not his permanent home. He was simply stationed here short term. "You'll be pleased to hear that I'm issuing you a babysitting hall pass when it comes to Madeline's care."

"You're mad at me."

"It was sweet of Theo to arrange backup for me, but I can handle Madeline by myself until

Theo and Aubrey come home."

He tilted his head. "You're mad at me," he repeated.

"I'm not invested enough to be mad." She sniffed. "I'm marginally perturbed at best."

He gave her a slow, lopsided smile, which immediately caused the backs of her knees to tingle. *Drat!*

"I want a second chance with you," he said.

"No, no." She spoke the words breezily. "There will be none of that. You and I have Theo in common and that's enough."

"Not for me."

"I'll be taking Madeline now. Good day to you, sir." She reached for the car seat, which he still held. But he didn't let go of its handle. She released her grip on it, drawing her brows together in frustration.

"I'll help you babysit Madeline," he said.

"No, indeed."

"It's what your brother wanted."

"And I'm using my veto power against my brother's wishes. I'll be caring for Madeline on my own. Most definitively."

"What if Theo has to stay overnight?"

"Then I'll care for her overnight."

"What if he has to stay here all day tomorrow?"

That gave her pause. She owned Polka-Dot Apron Pies, Misty River's first and only mobile pie shop. Tomorrow was Saturday, and Saturdays were busy. She'd need to begin baking in her commercial kitchen at seven thirty in the morning so that she could deliver the first round of pies to the camper trailer by opening time, at eleven.

"What time tomorrow do you need to get ready to go to work?" he asked, reading her mind.

"Six forty-five."

"Unless I hear from you or Theo between now and then, letting me know that something's changed, I'll take over for you with Madeline at six forty-five."

"Do you have experience with babies?"

"I just spent a month with my two infant nephews."

He was too polite to add, *and that makes me more qualified than you, Penelope.* Madeline was her first niece, which meant she had a sum total of a week and a half of aunt experience under her belt.

"If you end up staying with Madeline overnight, will you stay at your apartment or Theo's house?" he asked.

"Theo's house. May I have the baby seat

now?"

He set it on the ground. Since she was too nervous to attempt to carry a mini-human in one arm and a car seat in the other, she carefully laid the sleeping girl into the seat.

Madeline had been born with downy, light brown hair that stuck up at odd angles like ruffled bird feathers. In the way of newborns, she was gorgeous and, at the same time, slightly homely. Her forehead seemed to take up too much of the real estate on her face. This meant her eyes, nose, and mouth (which all appeared to be a size medium) had to jockey for space on the bottom half of her size-small head.

As Penelope wrestled with the seat's harness, Madeline stirred, her lips creasing with displeasure, her arms flashing outward. Penelope paused, biting her lip. Madeline, dressed in a lavender footed sleeper patterned with smiling panda faces, remained blessedly asleep. When Penelope finally slid the buckle into place it gave her finger a stinging pinch. She yelped and shook out her hand.

"Baby seat injury?" Eli asked mildly.

She had a wayward urge to push him and his handsome face and perfectly fitted shirt off the side of a waterfall.

"I can carry her to the car for you," he offered.

10

"Thanks, but no thanks. We're fine. Farewell, Eli." *Gah.* As she walked away, she forbid herself from sneaking one last, greedy peek at him.

As she ventured into the parking garage, she suddenly could see herself from the perspective of a camera zooming farther and farther away. Twenty-something woman of average height with slender limbs and curly brown hair, in charge of a helpless, fragile newborn baby. She'd done her best to project moxie to Eli. But in her own mind's eye, she looked intimidated and alone.

She shook her head to scatter the image. At the moment, she couldn't afford anything but confidence.

Wandering through the parking lot, she clicked the unlock button on Theo's key fob again and again until she finally pinpointed his car.

"Sorry about this, sweetheart, you adorable miniscule person you," she whispered to the sleeping baby as she turned the car seat this way and that, trying to attach it to the base. "Don't you worry. Auntie Penelope is going to figure this out and take good care of you until Mommy and Daddy come home. Ah." It clicked. "There. We're off."

She hurried around to the driver's seat and steered them toward Theo's house.

Penelope had been enamored with Madeline since the moment the infant had been placed in her arms. She'd stopped by Theo and Aubrey's house every day since. She'd wanted to be helpful, but so many grandparents had been on hand that showing up at her brother's house had been like showing up for a church project alongside five other volunteers for a job that only required one. She'd handled the baby just enough to know the basics of her care.

This was the first time Penelope had been solely responsible for the well-being of a child since her short-lived career as a babysitter in middle school. Back then, she'd sometimes become so immersed in the activities she'd started for the kids—craft projects, watercolor painting, walking the backyard in search of flowers—that she'd continued the projects after the kids lost interest, only to abruptly realize she had no idea where the children had gone. For the safety of all involved, it had been a *very* short-lived career.

She eased into Theo's cute neighborhood of pre–World War II homes and pulled into the garage of the two-bedroom, one-bathroom house he and Aubrey had purchased shortly after discovering they were expecting their first child. She toted Madeline into an interior Aubrey had decorated in farmhouse style—lots of white walls and warm wood. She'd just set the baby seat on the kitchen floor when her phone chimed.

A text from Theo. *The blood test and ultrasound confirm pulmonary embolism. She's stable, but this condition's serious. They're going to keep her overnight, at least. Can you stay with Madeline?*

Yes, absolutely.

Penelope tapped the toe of her Vans slip-ons and googled information on blood clots. Theo had been correct when he'd said that clotting occasionally happened to women after childbirth. Hospitalization was more likely for those who'd had surgery recently (Aubrey had had a C-section) and also for those with a family history of blood clotting.

Taking a deep breath, she considered the spiky rack that held clean bottles. Aubrey and Theo had been feeding the baby a combo of breastmilk and formula, so she had reason to hope Madeline would accept a bottle from her without a fuss. Carefully, she read the directions on the tub of formula. Once she'd washed her hands as thoroughly as a surgeon, she measured out the correct amount of water and mix so that she'd be ready to roll when Madeline woke.

In the nursey, she took a quick inventory, assuring herself that she knew where everything was located. Diapers, clean clothes, swaddling blankets, pacifiers. Check.

She gently freed Madeline from the seat. Still, her niece slept. This eight-and-a-half-pound, fully formed, perfect little human had no idea of the calamity that had overtaken her mom and dad.

Clasping Madeline in her arms, Penelope settled into a living room armchair and let her head tip against the chair's back.

Almost immediately, her exchange with Eli at the hospital slid to the forefront of her thoughts. Which, in turn, tugged her dating history forward.

Ricker, the Air Force base where Eli was stationed, was set like an apple in an upraised apron inside a valley embraced by some of North Georgia's tallest mountains. Misty River was situated on the far side of the valley, just twenty minutes from the base. With that kind of proximity and a population of only 5,500, her small town had always been impacted strongly by those who lived and worked at the base.

Mom, Dad, she, and Theo had followed Mom's banking job to Misty River around the time that Penelope entered middle school. At that age, she'd been oblivious to the handsome airmen walking

Misty River's streets. But a few years later, not so oblivious. She'd noticed them often—in the service dress light blue shirts and Air Force blue pants. Wearing camouflage combat dress. Leather flight jackets. Even in civilian clothing, one could spot them from a block away.

Her parents had informed her that, under no circumstances, was she allowed to date airmen. They were older, more experienced, and living free in the world without parental oversight.

She hadn't been a particularly obedient teenager. Her parents' rule against airmen might have backfired and made her determined to date them, except for two things.

One, the personalities of the airmen she met. Two, the way her friends reacted to them.

Air Force guys could be cocky, ambitious, and overserved with testosterone. Some were incapable of sharing softer feelings. Some refused to admit weakness. Also, they never stuck around for long. If you dated one of them, you'd spend a lot of time alone. If you married one of them, you'd face a higher divorce rate than the general population and you'd spend your life moving from place to place across the globe.

Even so, her group of friends, which had ranked three tiers down from the most popular group of girls at Misty River High School, had *adored* the airmen. They smiled at them with round cow eyes. They listened to them as if concert tickets were falling from their mouths. It seemed to Penelope that her friends' conduct inflated male egos already stretched at the seams like mylar balloons.

Whenever her friends turned right in unison, something within Penelope had *always* goaded her to turn left. One night in the spring semester of her junior year, she'd stood alone in the lobby of the movie theater, witnessing her friends' behavior. She'd been deeply embarrassed on their behalf, and in that moment, she'd determined that she would not follow the predictable path that they had chosen.

That same night, she'd announced to her friends that she would not date Air Force guys. She'd stuck to her guns easily through the remainder of high school and during the vacation time she'd spent at home while attending the University of North Georgia.

She tilted her profile down to study the nuances of Madeline's wrinkled, fisted hands. The little girl's scent of baby shampoo and milk drifted on the air.

After graduation, Penelope had moved into an

apartment in Misty River with her friend Lila and waited tables while looking for a permanent position in hospitality. Around that time, Lila had fallen madly in love with an Air Force Engineering Officer named Brady. They'd been euphorically happy right up until he deployed to the Middle East. Penelope held Lila's hand through misery over their separation that was every bit as low as the euphoria had been high while privately doubting whether Brady was fit to shine Lila's shoes.

Brady eventually returned. Lila was euphoric again. But soon after, miserable again. Only later did Lila tell Penelope that she'd gotten pregnant and gone alone to a clinic for an abortion.

Brady had eventually been restationed to Hawaii. Maintaining a long-distance relationship proved too hard for the couple, and Brady broke up with Lila. Penelope mopped Lila's tears.

She mopped Destiny's tears when Carter was injured and chose to return home free of both his military responsibilities and Destiny. She mopped Jennifer's tears when Brett deployed. She mopped Gabby's tears after her divorce from Nathan. She mopped Peyton's tears when Brandon's squadron was sent to California. She mopped Michelle's tears when Carlos behaved like a punk.

As far as she could tell, all of her friends had surrendered their identities to the heroic, high-stakes professions of their significant others, which *galled* Penelope. Her individuality was her most precious commodity.

For ten years, she'd not once violated her rule against dating airmen.

And then, a year and a half ago, her beloved brother had befriended Captain Eli Joseph Price, call sign Big Sky.

And Eli was . . . great.

Eli had thrown into doubt all the stereotypes she'd constructed.

Eli had tempted her into bending her rule.

Chapter Two

Looking for Penelope had become a habit Eli couldn't break.

A few months before he'd left Georgia, he'd started looking for her everywhere he went in Misty River, like a TV antenna trying to pick up a signal.

He'd continued to look for her when he'd been half a world away. It had made no sense, but he'd climb from the cockpit of his F-22 and catch himself scanning the horizon for a red '74 Bronco. In meetings, he'd hear the door open and glance up, hoping it was her. When he downloaded email, he looked for her name.

Finally, this evening, he'd come face-to-face with her again. She was angry with him, but he'd been so overwhelmingly glad to see her that even her irritation hadn't had the power to ruin his mood.

At Ricker's gate, he slowed his black '70 Mustang and showed his ID. The SPs waved him forward.

Soon after Penelope had rejected his help with Madeline, he'd received a text from a buddy, letting him know that he was scheduled to lead mission on Monday. He'd decided to stop by the squadron to check the flying schedule in order to give himself additional time to prepare. He continued past the turnoff he'd have taken to reach his apartment.

When he'd come to Georgia, he'd moved into bachelor officer's quarters on base without even bothering to paint the apartment's beige walls. At his base in Alaska, and in Florida before that, he'd chosen equally simple housing. Avoiding a commute to work was worth more to him than either the comfort or impressiveness of the housing choices in town.

Other than a few pieces of modern art painted by an artist from Montana, his top-of-the-line television, and his sound system, he didn't have a lot. Just clothes, bedding, sports equipment, and his car.

He'd never needed much beyond flying. Flying was the center of almost everything he thought about and did and cared about, and had been since his parents had taken him and his older and younger brothers to a Thunderbirds demonstration when he'd been in third grade.

In fact, flying had been enough for him right up until Penelope Quinn had entered his life like the asteroid that killed the dinosaurs.

Inside the squadron, he spent time shaking hands and catching up with the squadron intel officer and an exec he hadn't seen since he'd left for Syria. Then he made his way into the scheduling shop, where the flying schedule filled a large whiteboard. He noted the flight's call sign and information, then frowned slightly at the names of his wingmen, who were good but not quite up to his standards. He took his time studying the takeoff and landing times, aircraft configuration, operating area, and the list of additional assets they'd be working with.

Eventually, he caught himself staring at the board without seeing it. Instead, Penelope filled his mind.

Earlier, her skin had looked lightly tanned. It was summer, so a tan was expected. But he knew her skin looked that same way even in the middle of winter. Tiny freckles were sprinkled across her nose, cheekbones, and beneath the graceful lines of her eyebrows. She had an expressive mouth and slate blue eyes.

Her hair was mostly caramel brown in color, but lightened here and there by strands of dark gold. She wore it in long, natural waves that always reminded him of a day at the beach even though they were hundreds of miles from the nearest coast.

He'd been drawn to her because of their similarities—their sense of humor, their faith, the importance they placed on their family. And because of their differences, too. He was factual and she was creative. He was strait-laced and she was quirky. He was a rule-follower and there was something just a little bit reckless about Penelope.

At last, he'd returned to Georgia. At last, he had an opportunity to convince her to give him a second chance.

●　　●　　●

Keeping a newborn alive through the night made for seriously subpar sleep. Penelope had been awakened by Madeline three—or was it four?—times. There wasn't enough iced tea in the world to vanquish the level of exhaustion she was experiencing this morning. It weighted her limbs and stuffed her head with wool.

Since she'd had no overnight bag, she'd made do by finger-brushing toothpaste onto her teeth last night and this morning, borrowing Aubrey's face wash, and donning a yoga pants/exercise top set this morning that she'd found at the bottom of Aubrey's drawer beneath pregnancy workout gear. Her hair was a tangle and she couldn't wait to return to her own shower, clothing, and cosmetics.

At six forty-five, the doorbell rang and she swung the front door wide.

She found Eli standing on the threshold, hands in the pockets of his jeans. The name of his favorite band, The Cranberries, was written across his ivory T-shirt in washed-out gray.

A warm, melting sensation swirled within her torso. "You're here," she said. *What an astonishing observation, Penelope. So astute!*

"I am."

The glitter of morning sunlight against glossy paint drew her focus to his Mustang parked on the curb. He'd purchased it from his grandfather, who restored classic cars. She, too, owned a '70s Ford, which she'd once taken as a sign from heaven that a romance between them was destined.

"Come on in." She held the door as he passed through.

"How'd it go last night?" he asked.

"I think it went fairly normally for Madeline, but I feel as though I've been hit in the face with a frying pan." She led him into the living room. "She's currently relaxing in this Moses basket type thing."

"Is that for babies? It looks like something that should hold magazines."

"I'm ninety percent sure it's for babies."

He lifted the basket. Turning it to face him, he contemplated the infant with a small, smitten smile that had the power to twist her resolve into a pretzel.

"Morning," he said to Madeline. "It's a pleasure to see you again."

Madeline, swaddled snuggly in a pink blanket, regarded him with wise eyes.

Penelope swept around the space, bringing him up to speed on all aspects of Madeline's care. Any sensible single, childless, thirty-year-old man should be daunted at the task he was about to undertake. But he did not appear daunted.

She paused in the foyer before leaving. "Are you two going to be okay?"

"We're going to be fine."

"Any questions for me?"

"Nope. I've got this."

Her lips curved. "Funny, that's exactly what I said to Theo yesterday before I took over with Madeline."

"But today you feel like you've been hit in the face with a frying pan."

"Precisely. Naivety can be so empowering."

He lifted a strong shoulder and smiled. "I guess it's my turn to get hit in the face with a frying pan. You're needed elsewhere. If Polka-Dot Apron Pies doesn't open today, we'll have an angry mob on our hands."

"My car's still at the hospital, so I'm taking Theo's car. Last I heard, Theo's planning to Uber here around lunchtime to clean up and gather Aubrey's things. Then he's going to take Madeline up to the hospital with him in Aubrey's car."

He nodded. The air between them thickened.

"Penelope," he started, "I—"

"Some of Aubrey's friends are scheduled to watch Madeline tonight. After that, we'll play it by ear. And now I'm off." But then she stilled uncertainly halfway through the doorway. "Sure you don't have any questions?"

"Just one."

"Which is?"

"When are we going to talk about us? Because that needs to happen—"

"Never?" she proposed.

At the same moment he said, "Soon."

"Good day to you!"

"*Soon*," she heard him reiterate in the split second before the door closed behind her.

• • •

When Eli arrived at Misty River's sports complex that afternoon to coach Theo's basketball team, he immediately discovered two things. One, the team was called the Sharpshooters. Two, they were *not* sharpshooters.

He stood on the indoor court they'd been assigned, guiding them through a warm-up before their game, torn between humor and pity. The boys were small and skinny, uncoordinated and tentative. Typically, on elementary school teams, at least one or two of the kids was an unusually good athlete and the good athletes carried the rest. But all the players on this team only seemed good at dressing themselves in their spotless bright red uniforms and remembering to bring water bottles.

The assistant coach, a preppy dad who'd introduced himself as Creighton, paced along the baseline while talking on his phone.

When the buzzer sounded to indicate that their warm-up had concluded, Eli called, "Huddle up."

Creighton held up a finger, pointed to his phone, and turned his back in order to continue his conversation.

The boys obediently trotted to Eli. One of them tripped over his own feet and landed on all fours, but he quickly popped back up and continued forward. They circled around Eli, a group of unbelievably short kids.

"Who's ready to play some basketball?" Eli asked.

"Me," they all said sweetly.

None of them had the eye of the tiger. "Which five of you usually start a game?"

Eight of the ten kids raised their hands. *Great.* "Of those of you who have your hand raised, who plays guard?"

Three kept their hands in the air. "Okay. You and you will be our starting guards. You and you will play forward, and you will play center. Everybody clear on their roles?"

One kid made an "Mm-mm" sound. The starters nodded vaguely. The non-starters looked disappointed and resigned.

"Has Coach Theo taught you some plays?"

"We got three plays," a dark-haired kid said. "Lion, cobra, and . . ." He screwed up his face.

"Shark," another kid supplied. He jerked his bony hips from side to side and sang, "Baby shark, doo doo doo doo doo doo."

A few of the other kids joined in the singing and dancing and Eli had to work to recapture their attention. "Do you have hand signals for the plays?" Eli asked the guards.

"Yeah."

"Whichever of you brings down the ball, make sure you signal the play to the rest of the team." He continued to give instructions, but only one freckle-faced boy seemed to be paying close attention. A few were more interested in the light fixtures above. Some were studying the girls' game that had just started on the next court over. One was fascinated with a loose thread on his waistband.

Eli extended his hand to the middle of the circle and the kids jostled forward to stack their hands on top of his. "Sharpshooters on three," Eli said. "One, two . . ."

"Sharpshooters!"

Play began. It looked more like a frantic wrestling match than the sport of basketball. None of his players secured a rebound. The one kid who attempted a rebound whiffed the ball, which clunked off his forehead. He came out crying. Most of the time the guards forgot to signal the play and, when they did remember, none of their teammates was paying attention.

At halftime, Eli looked around for his assistant coach. Creighton again raised his finger and pointed at his phone. So Eli took it upon himself to give the boys an inspiring speech about basketball strategy. They listened with blank boredom. He finished with, "Let's play hard, play clean, and give it our all."

"Can I use the bathroom?" one of them asked.

"I think I broke my ankle," another stated.

Creighton wandered over, clapped three times, and said, "Hustle out there, guys. *Hustle!*"

It was a massacre. So much so that a wave of relief washed through Eli when the final buzzer sounded.

"What's the team's win–loss record this season?" Eli asked Creighton, who was gathering the basketballs into a large bag.

"No wins. Just losses."

Theo was having a terrible week. The least Eli could do for his friend was knock the substitute coaching role Theo had given him out of the park. Today he'd been, at best, a mediocre coach.

He could do better.

The boys' parents brought their sons over one by one to tell him thank you. As he shook small hands, gave out fist bumps, and returned high fives, Eli made up his mind.

He was going to do whatever he could to ensure that the not-so-Sharpshooters brought home a win.

Chapter Three

Widely accepted truth: When your family members are going through a health crisis, it's important to be as stoic and dependable as the Rock of Gibraltar.

This was an axiom Penelope wholeheartedly subscribed to. Yet when she entered Aubrey's hospital room after work on Saturday, she burst into tears at the sight of Aubrey in her hospital bed.

"Pen," Theo murmured kindly, standing to hug her. Gray circles smudged the skin beneath his eyes. "Are you all right?"

"I'm fine!" Penelope's voice wobbled like a brand-new ice skater. Tears gushed over her lashes. "Just fine!" Also, potentially mentally unstable.

"Aww," Aubrey said to Penelope. "C'mere." In one arm, she cradled a sleeping Madeline. She extended her other arm to Penelope.

Penelope intertwined her fingers with Aubrey's

and squeezed. "How are you?"

"Better than I was yesterday." Aubrey, a true Southern lady, did not resemble her ladylike self at present. She'd gathered her blond hair in a messy ponytail. Much of her usual color was missing from her oval face. With an IV and monitors attached to her, she seemed frail. Vulnerable. Her poor body had barely begun to recover from the C-section when she'd received this second enormous physical blow in the form of a blood clot.

Separating from Aubrey, Penelope made an urgent grab for the box of Kleenex near the sink, then blew her nose.

"You're sleep-deprived, aren't you?" Aubrey said. "I recognize the symptoms."

"I'm fine! I did get some"—*hardly any*—"sleep last night."

"Little-known fact about me," Theo said. "I burst into tears myself the day after we brought Madeline home from the hospital."

Aubrey smiled. "No, he didn't."

"I don't seem to be able to make it stop." Penelope gestured irritably with a fresh tissue. "I so wanted to be the Rock of Gibraltar!"

They regarded her with confusion. "Why would you want to be the Rock of Gibraltar?" Theo asked.

"So many reasons!" Penelope wailed.

Theo put an arm around her shoulders. "Let's step outside and take a breather."

"'Kay."

"Thank you for keeping Madeline last night," Aubrey said to her.

"Of course. I adore Madeline and I want to help you guys any way I can."

Theo steered her from the room and down the hallway to an alcove housing vending machines. He bought her a Snickers, her favorite candy bar. His favorite was Heath bar, which was why she'd named the Heath-bar-inspired pie on her menu "Theo's Pie."

They leaned, side by side, against a white patch of wall. A leggy brother and sister with matching brown curls that they'd inherited from their mother.

Her crying drifted away like a summer storm while she chewed her Snickers.

She'd won the sibling contest when God gave her Theo. He was three years older and, while she'd annoyed him when he was in middle school and hardly seen him when he was in high school, their vibe had never turned seriously rocky because Theo was good-hearted to the bone.

"What are the doctors saying about Aubrey?"

she asked.

"Well, first of all, they're taking great care of her here."

"Good."

"But, unfortunately, her risk factors make treatment complicated. She'll need to stay here a couple more days, at least."

"What are they giving her to treat the blood clot?"

"Blood thinners and clot dissolvers. For now, it looks like those might be sufficient. If not, they'll thread a catheter through her blood vessels."

"Yikes."

"My focus right now is to get Aubrey and Madeline through this as smoothly as possible."

"You're going to need a lot of help."

"Agreed."

"And you have to take care of yourself, too. Can your employees at Blue Ridge Adventures cover your workload?"

"It won't be easy, but over the short term—yes."

"Okay, then I want you to prioritize sleep, food, water, rest. If you don't, you're going to start to fall apart. And that, we cannot have."

He grunted.

"No, really." She spoke in her sternest voice.

"Tomorrow's my day off and my work schedule is flexible, so I'm depending on you to rely on me as much as you need."

He bumped his shoulder against hers affectionately. "Thank you."

"If you need them, Mom and Dad will come back to help, too." Four years ago, their parents had once again followed a job offer Mom had received and relocated to Boston. By then, Theo and Penelope both considered Misty River home. The two of them had stayed.

"I know. I'm not ready to ask them to do that yet. They took off work to be here last week."

She peeled the wrapper farther down her candy bar. "So. How did Eli do taking care of Madeline today?"

"Great. I was later getting to the house than expected because I waited with Aubrey to talk to her doctor. When I got there, everything was clean and quiet. Madeline was sleeping and he was watching baseball."

"Huh."

"He didn't burst into tears."

"Touché."

"Is something going on between you two?" This wasn't the first time over the past eighteen months that he'd asked the question.

34

"Nope."

"Would you tell me if there was?"

"Nope."

"He likes you."

"I don't date Air Force guys."

"He's a much better catch than Cameron."

Over the past month, she'd gone on three dates with Cameron Kaplinsky, computer programmer. "You're not the one going on dates with Cameron, so your opinion hardly qualifies."

"I'm your doting older brother who cares about your happiness. My opinion should qualify."

"No, indeed." She finished her Snickers. "Hit me again, please."

His brows rose. "A double?"

"It's been a long day."

He slid coins into the vending machine and handed her a second Snickers.

"Just between you and me, it's nice to take a break from that hospital room for a minute." He resumed his position against the wall next to her and clicked through apps on his phone.

She remained beside him, offering silent companionship and tasting chewy caramel, chocolate, and peanuts.

Theo had started his own adventure tour business several years ago. He and his three staffers took people on hiking, paddling, and fishing expeditions that lasted anywhere from a day to a week.

Shortly after Eli had arrived at Ricker, he'd stopped by Theo's business. Eli loved to fish and had signed up for a two-day fishing weekend Theo had led. The two had come back from the trip besties.

Eli had joined Theo's weekly basketball game at the gym and, soon after, Theo had introduced Eli to Penelope at a party. Penelope's rapport with Eli had been *instantaneously* good. He knew when to listen. He knew when to extend sympathy and when to deliver a joke. And he appreciated her just the way she was.

His easy-going demeanor could fool you into thinking he was low-key through and through. However, she'd learned that a smart, high-powered engine hummed beneath his exterior. If you looked closely enough into his eyes, you could see banked intensity smoldering there. Eli was driven. He'd entered the Air Force Academy out of high school, earned excellent grades, and eventually achieved his boyhood dream of piloting fighter jets. She'd learned from Eli's Air Force friends that Eli possessed a legendary combination of nerves, reflexes, talent, and focus—all of which made him perfectly suited for his job.

Because she and Eli were both in Theo's solar system, they'd continued to see each other often socially. Whenever they did, they joked and laughed and bantered.

Over a period of months, it had occurred to her that Eli might be just what she'd been hoping to find—a successful, honorable man whose faith was important to him.

Nine months ago, he'd started asking her out. She explained her rule and regretfully turned him down. Their paths continued to cross. He continued to ask her out. For the next three months, she continued to say no even as the chemistry and fondness between them mounted sweetly higher and higher.

Penelope's friends and family liked to tease her about her tendency to get "too wrapped up" in things. At the age of seven, she'd famously gotten wrapped up in Legos and created masterworks that stretched from the floor to her bedroom ceiling. Since then, she'd become obsessed with the country of France, painting with watercolors, playing the violin, songwriting, Himalayan cats, Ford Broncos, and, most recently, pie-making. Each of these eras had lasted for years at a time.

She viewed her ability to immerse herself in a pursuit as an asset. However, she could admit that making Eli into her newest obsession *was not wise.* She refused to become the gullible local girl. She would not surrender who she was at the throne of his career, then weep tears over him her friends had to mop.

Also, she suspected that he could not possibly be as decent and trustworthy as he seemed to be. So she hunted for evidence to support her suspicion. When the other shoe dropped, she planned to point to it and crow, "Ah-ha! I knew dating you would be a terrible idea!"

Theo gave a weary grunt as he straightened. "I'm going back in."

"I'm coming with."

She chatted with Aubrey for thirty minutes, then drove her own car to her apartment, located on the second floor of one of the historic commercial buildings near the grassy park at the heart of Misty River's downtown.

When she entered the space, her Himalayan cat greeted her by weaving through her legs. She lifted him and gave him a thorough head rub. "Greetings, Roy."

As always, her cheery, light-filled apartment surrounded her with comfort. Ferns, ivy, violets, and cyclamen lent bursts of color. Bookcases stuffed with volumes on cooking, music, and art lined several of the walls. She'd decorated the space with an eclectic mix of furnishings and artwork she'd scored at flea markets.

She loved living within walking distance of many of Misty River's restaurants and shops. In fact, her relationship with Eli had come to a head six months ago, precisely because they'd attended a group dinner at a restaurant a few blocks from here and, afterward, he'd learned that she intended to walk home.

She set Roy on his feet and began the process of making iced tea.

On that long-ago night, as she'd donned mittens, a hat, and a scarf, Eli had offered to give her a ride home. She'd told him that she preferred to walk. At which time, he'd said he wanted to walk with her. At which time, she'd told him that would be acceptable.

They'd taken the riverwalk, deserted at that late and frigid hour. While they'd chatted companionably, she'd snuck glances at him when he wasn't looking. As they approached Midnight Ranch, the sound of live country music tumbled from the bar. The lyrics of an old, familiar song by Lonestar reached her. *I don't know how you do what you do. I'm so in love with you . . .*

They passed by and the music was lessening slightly in volume when they reached a small courtyard framed by winter flowers and dark businesses.

"May I have this dance?" he'd asked her.

Her caution whispered *no*, but her mouth said, "Yes."

She placed her hand in his and her skin rushed with heat. Chuckling, they stopped and started a few times before finding the rhythm of the two-step. They made slow circles around the court-yard—a private, moonlit dance.

"Your stairs playground me," he mumble-sang under his breath. "Baby, you astound me."

Her laughter rang clear in the cold air. "'Your hair all around me,'" she corrected. "'Baby, you surround me.'"

The few times they'd attempted karaoke with mutual friends, she'd cajoled him into singing "You've Lost That Lovin' Feelin'," the song Tom Cruise had immortalized in *Top Gun*. Even with the lyrics on a screen in front of him, Eli's attention would wander, and he'd end up fudging some of the words. He was a lost cause with lyrics.

"But you do astound me," he pointed out rea-sonably. "The words should be 'baby, you astound me.'"

"And do you also contend that 'your stairs playground me' is a superior lyric?"

"I admit that one leaves a little to be desired."

He spun her and she came to a stop flush against the front of his jacket. The motion between them ceased and their teasing melted into seriousness.

He looked at her with so much tenderness that it stole her breath.

His head bent toward hers. He paused, halfway, his gaze searching. The yes/no battle she'd been feeling toward him for weeks continued to rage in her mind even as her body rushed with ecstatic anticipation.

When his lips took hers, she curved her fingers into his down jacket. His arms banded behind her. They kissed like they were the last two people on earth and they had five minutes left to live.

Her blood roared. Possessiveness of him, adoration of him swamped her. As did the delicious scent and taste and feel of him.

It was the first time they kissed, and it was—by light-years—the best kiss of her life.

They'd held hands the rest of the way to her apartment. At the front door of her building, he'd asked again if she'd go out with him. She'd told him she'd consider it with great seriousness.

Penelope poured the iced tea into a huge glass of ice and sat at her small kitchen table illuminated by a slant of sunlight. Roy jumped onto her lap and provided a cat massage by kneading her thigh. Sighing, she drank half the glass in one long pull.

The day after she'd kissed Eli, she'd floated through her duties at the pie truck on leftover adrenaline. She'd been fairly certain that, in Eli, she'd found the man who'd make the setting aside of her long-held, well-known rule worthwhile.

Then one of her regulars had arrived at Polka-Dot Apron Pies with an appetite and news. Jodi was in her early forties and had been married to Chris, Eli's squadron boss, for twenty years.

"I'm hoping to get Chris out here for one last slice of pecan pie before they go," Jodi said to Penelope.

Foreboding skittered between Penelope's shoulder blades. "Go?"

"To Syria."

"Hmm?"

"The squadron's leaving for Syria in three days. Sorry, I thought I'd mentioned it."

Eli was leaving for Syria in three days? "When . . ." With effort, she cleared her throat. "When did the squadron find out that they're deploying?"

"A few months back."

Standing in her pie truck, looking into Jodi's kindly face, the other shoe had, at last, dropped. But she didn't feel like crowing, "Ah-ha! I knew that dating you would be a terrible idea!" because she was so wretchedly disappointed.

Instead of finding out from the man she'd just kissed that he was departing for Syria, she'd found out from a customer.

She'd given herself the rest of that workday to gather her composure, then called Eli as soon as she'd returned to her apartment. Pacing, she listened to the phone ring.

"Hey," he said warmly. "I'm glad you called, I was just thinking about you—"

"Jodi told me that you're leaving for Syria in three days."

Silence.

"Is that true?" she pressed.

"Yeah," he admitted after a few more seconds had passed. "Look, I should have said something sooner."

"I really would have appreciated it if you had." She'd thought she had her temper under control. But now the sound of his voice was stirring her anger the way hurricane winds stir deep ocean.

"As it is, you didn't give me full information and so I feel, well . . . tricked into last night's kiss."

"I didn't trick you."

"Didn't you? You weren't truthful with me."

"I was going to tell you myself, my own way. I'm sorry. Let me take you out for dinner. We can—"

"No." She spoke calmly, but also emphatically. For the first time ever, she'd made an exception to her rule. For him. And now this!

She wanted to kill him. But only hypothetically. There was nothing hypothetical about the dangers he'd be facing overseas. This was likely the last communication they'd have before he shipped off to a war zone. Her conscience wouldn't allow her to unleash her indignation on him at this point because . . . what if something happened to him? "You're headed to Syria and that's going to require all of your focus."

"But not every minute of my time. We can keep in touch by email and occasionally by phone while I'm gone."

"I'd prefer not to."

"Why?"

"Last night's kiss was a mistake." In fact, she bitterly regretted it already.

In the quiet that followed, Roy meowed twice.

"We'll remain friends," she said in a bracing tone. "I wish you a safe and successful deployment—"

"Penelope—"

"I'll see you when you return."

She'd wrapped up their phone call as quickly as possible.

He'd respected her wishes and refrained from reaching out to her while he was in Syria.

Penelope had moved on, her individuality and freedom intact. Frequently, she'd told herself she should feel fortunate to have escaped such a near miss.

As far as Theo and her friends were concerned, the kiss hadn't happened because she'd never told any of them about it. Penelope herself often wished that it hadn't happened. As it was, she remembered their kiss often. When falling asleep at night. When rolling out pie dough. When sitting across a dinner table from Cameron Kaplinsky.

And every time, the memory of it made her wayward heart beat faster.

Chapter Four

Madeline was screaming. Eli immediately registered both that fact and Penelope's tight expression when he arrived at Theo's house the next night around dinnertime.

"Any chance you can make this stop?" She motioned to the red-faced infant in her arms.

"I can try." Eli stepped inside and set down the white paper sack full of food he'd brought. The moment he'd learned from Theo that his shift would follow Penelope's this evening, he'd decided to buy dinner for Penelope and himself. He was hoping the meal would convince her to stick around long enough to talk.

Eagerly, she passed Madeline to him.

He held the furious child around the torso with both hands, studying her with sympathy. "Bad day?"

"Yes," Penelope answered.

Madeline wailed.

He pressed Madeline against his shoulder, rocking slowly, trying to calm her while studying Penelope. She wore a navy-and-white-striped dress that looked like a long T-shirt. The plain white slip-on Vans she'd chosen meant she'd been feeling practical this morning. Her beachy hair was all over the place. Pink colored her cheeks beneath her tan.

This was the third time in three days that they'd come face-to-face. The power of her nearness hadn't lessened. When he was within thirty feet of her, it was like he was incapable of concentrating on anything *but* her. Even crying babies. "Um." *Focus, Eli.* "What usually works with Madeline in this scenario?"

"Swaddle, clean diaper, pacifier, or bottle. She got angry when I was giving her a bath a little while ago. I've tried all the usual approaches and none of them are working. I'm worried I'm doing something wrong." She filled her cheeks with air, then pushed it out in a frazzled breath.

"If you had to guess, what would you say is the matter?"

"Madeline's deep hatred of baths?"

"Any other ideas?"

"It's possible that I might not have burped her as well as I should have the last time I gave her a bottle."

Eli placed the heel of his hand at the base of Madeline's spine, then pressed it up her back in careful circles. "This is my brother's technique."

"If this technique stops her crying, I shall be overwhelmed with admiration for your brother."

He circled his hand up her back several more times without success. "Do you have a blanket nearby?"

He knelt on the living room rug while Penelope retrieved it. Without having to ask, she placed the blanket on the floor in the swaddling-ready position. He lowered the screaming girl onto it, then wrapped her securely.

Madeline's eyes rounded with outrage. More bawling.

"She knows we're not Mom and Dad and that this situation is jacked up," Penelope stated.

"Does she have one of those, you know"—he held his arm at a diagonal angle—"baby seat things?"

"Yes."

"If you'll go get it, Madeline and I will meet you in the laundry room."

"I will not allow you to place my niece in the washing machine."

He laughed. "Meet us in the laundry room."

Inside the small space, he cleared items off the dryer, then turned it on.

Penelope arrived with the seat. "Are you wanting me to set this on top?"

"Yes, please."

She did so. "Is this another of your brother's techniques?"

"Yep."

They worked together to snap the sobbing baby into the seat.

"This is what happens," Penelope whispered, "when two sane, responsible parents leave their child in the care of an aunt who bakes pies and a fighter pilot."

"If we can bake pies and fly planes, we can handle this."

"Naivety is empowering." She repeated her statement from yesterday, then tipped a wry look at her niece. "That's Madeline's why-did-you-rookies-put-me-on-the-dryer face."

"Pacifier, please."

"Are you now the baby happiness doctor? I'm her aunt, so I should be the doctor. You should be my nurse."

"This is no time to protest this hospital's hierarchy." Humor curved his lips.

She darted away. Moments later, she handed

him a pacifier. Over and over again, he tried to get Madeline to take it. She kept refusing, but the dryer's sound and vibration did seem to be calming her a little. On his tenth attempt to interest her in the pacifier, she finally accepted it.

"That a girl." Eli kept his fingertip on the pacifier's end, whispering lullaby words. "Cat in the cradle . . . Peter pumpkin eater . . . The dish ran away with the spoon."

Penelope sank onto the laundry room's wooden stool. "Thank you Father, Son, and Holy Ghost. Quiet has never sounded so sweet."

Madeline sucked her pacifier with rhythmic concentration, her watery eyes wide open.

"That's her you're-so-unorthodox-that-I've-decided-to-give-you-brownie-points-for-creativity face," Eli said.

When Penelope didn't reply, he glanced at her and caught her staring at him as if in the middle of a daydream. "I . . ." She clicked her teeth together and said nothing more.

"In case you're hungry, I brought dinner," he told her. "It's from The Junction."

"Fried chicken, mashed potatoes, green beans, bread?" she asked hopefully. Old-fashioned, Southern comfort food was her favorite.

"You got it."

"Bless your soul. I'll start getting it ready."

"I'd help but—"

"You have your finger on a crack in a dam. I'd prefer you not move until she's asleep."

Madeline's eyelids grew heavier.

"That's her now-that-awesome-Eli-is-here-I-can-sleep face," he said.

"That's also her you-two-are-so-inept-that-you've-tired-me-out face."

Madeline's lids drifted closed. The noise of her drawing on her pacifier continued.

"That's her I'm-dreaming-of-returning-to-the-womb face," Penelope said.

"It's also her I'm-imagining-my-future-career-as-a-pilot face."

"It's also her I-adore-my-aunt-Penelope-and-will-one-day-apologize-to-her-for-my-tantrum-by-buying-her-peppermint-gelato face."

"I'll buy you peppermint gelato," he said.

She vanished into the kitchen.

He stayed in the laundry room with Madeline for several more minutes. Then, unwilling to risk removing the baby from the seat, carried the entire thing to the dining room.

"She looks like a really tired Cleopatra on a litter," Penelope remarked.

He saw that Penelope had set the table, filled

their plates with food and their glasses with tea. He placed the baby seat on the floor near their chairs as carefully as if it contained plutonium.

Madeline continued sleeping.

He took his seat. Penelope said a prayer, then they started in on the meal.

Distantly, he could tell that it tasted good. It was hard to concentrate on flavors when Penelope Quinn was seated next to him.

"I'd like to know what it was like for you, over in Syria," she said. "Would you be willing to talk with me about it?"

"Sure."

She asked curious questions, and he answered her as thoroughly as security restrictions allowed.

"Can you give me a sense of what a normal work week in Syria was like?" She took a bite of potatoes.

"We're constantly going through a rolling process. We're given a mission objective. We plan. We perform the mission. Debrief. More intelligence is gathered. We're given another mission—"

Madeline made a sound and they both froze.

The pacifier popped onto her blanket. Eli put his reflexes to work by leaning down to retrieve and reinsert.

Success. The baby's head slumped to the side in

sleep.

"That's her I-thought-it-would-be-fun-to-scare-you-because-I-don't-want-you-to-get-too-comfortable face," Penelope said softly.

"That's her you-guys-fell-for-it face." He grinned at Penelope over their running joke.

She smiled back at him for a split second, then looked away. The amusement in her face disappeared.

He cursed inwardly and set down his fork. He hated that he'd hurt her before he'd left for Syria.

She rose. "More butter for your roll?"

"No, thanks."

He rose, too. After straightening his gray shirt, he thrust his hands into the pockets of his faded jeans. "I'm sorry I didn't tell you I was being deployed."

She paused in the act of removing the butter from the fridge. Then continued her movement, setting the dish on the counter, closing the refrigerator door. Finally, she met his eyes, her face carefully neutral.

"I liked you from the first day we met," he said. "The more I got to know you, the more I liked you. You're the Picasso of pie. You're devoted to your family. You crack jokes that make me laugh. You love your cat. I don't know anyone in the world like you . . . and I mean that as a compliment."

"I'll take it as a compliment." She set a hip against the counter and loosely crossed her arms. It was a casual pose, but he could read caution in the angle of her jaw.

"But I couldn't convince you to go out with me," he said, "because of your rule."

"I know you think my rule's unfair. However, I have ten years of experience to back up its validity."

"Actually, I think half of the reason for your rule *is* fair. You're right about the fact that any Air Force boyfriend of yours would have to leave for months at a time and have to move often. None of that can be changed."

"I wouldn't ask anyone to change it. What you do is hugely important, Eli. I respect it. And I fully support it."

But his job didn't make him good boyfriend material. He understood, very well, why that was the case. A few years from now, he hoped to make Major. He was committed to defending his country, which meant that any girlfriend of his would have to make big sacrifices because of his commitment.

"The other half of the reason for my rule is also

fair," she said.

He already had a lot to overcome with her because of his career. So it made him crazy that the lousy behavior of Penelope's friends' boyfriends had hurt his chances further. "I admit that I've known plenty of Air Force guys who have the type of personality you don't want—arrogant, selfish, ambitious. The problem is, that's a stereotype and stereotypes are often liars. I've known a lot of guys who are nothing like that. *I'm* nothing like that. Which is what I was trying to show you before I deployed."

She cocked her head. "But then you lied to me by omission by not telling me about Syria."

"Which was a mistake. I should have told you. I didn't because I worried that you wouldn't give me a chance if you found out I was about to go."

She had an unforgettable face, powerfully beautiful. "Instead of predicting my response, it would have been better to tell me honestly about the deployment, then let *me* decide on my response."

"You're right." Pressure built inside his head because he wanted so badly to get this right with her. "I didn't want to lose you so I said nothing."

"And your strategy worked. You kept Syria a secret and I kissed you. But you won a battle only to lose the war because Jodi came to the pie shop the next day and told me about Syria. In that moment, I felt like I'd been used, the same way my friends had been used." She pushed one of the long, wavy strands of her hair out of her face. "Years ago, I promised myself that I wasn't going to get played by any of you. And then I got played. It was humiliating because it made me feel like the easy-to-manipulate hometown girl I'd never wanted to be."

"I screwed up and I'm sorry. I've regretted the way I handled that for the last six months."

"Well," she said lightly, waving a hand. "No doubt, because of Theo, we'll see each other a lot before you're sent to another base." She carried the butter to the table, took her seat. "We can be friends."

"I want to be more than friends." He remained standing.

"I don't think that's a good idea."

"Why?"

"Well, for one thing, while you were away, I started dating someone else."

His body turned to stone. "Who?"

"Cameron Kaplinsky."

He bent stiffly into his chair. His brain had turned the color black. He'd known, of course, that she might find someone else while he was gone. If that happened, he'd thought Theo would tell him. Because Theo hadn't said anything, he'd assumed he was in the clear. "Is Cameron the guy who was at Peyton's Christmas party? The computer programmer?"

"One and the same." She continued with her meal.

His hands remained motionless on his thighs. "He's not good enough for you."

"I think he is."

"No. How long have you been dating him?"

"A month."

"Is it serious?"

"No."

"Exclusive?"

"No."

Thank God. "What can I do to convince you to date me instead of him?"

"I don't date Air Force—"

"Penelope."

"Yes?"

"Can you try for just one minute not to paint me with the same brush as your friends' boy-friends?" he asked calmly. "What concerns do you have that *aren't* about my job? What concerns do you have that are just about *me*?" He flattened a hand against his chest.

"That ship has sailed—"

"We're not over. We haven't even gotten started. What are your concerns?"

Several seconds passed.

He adored everything about her, and he couldn't remember when something had been as important to him as this was.

"I'm concerned that I can't count on you to be truthful," she said at last. "I don't want to be manipulated."

"And?"

"I'm concerned that you're too macho to communicate your feelings."

"And?"

"I'm concerned that you're not the type of guy who, I don't know . . . would be willing to make a fool of himself for love. You're so self-possessed all the time."

"And?"

"That's it."

"Okay."

She tilted her head. "*Now* do you agree that we shouldn't date?"

"There's nothing on this earth," he told her firmly, "that I disagree with more strongly than the idea that we should not date."

Chapter Five

The F-22 became an extension of Eli when he flew it. Yet the plane also reminded him, every time, that he was the most fragile, mistake-prone part of the machine.

On Monday morning, just after take-off, Eli hauled the jet up, planted a turn, then streaked cleanly into the sky.

The F-22 Raptor was a weapon built for war. A single-seat, two-engine stealth tactical fighter constructed by Lockheed Martin for the Air Force at a cost of 150 million dollars each. Top speed: fifteen hundred miles per hour.

Its raw power could push him down into his ejection seat at nine times his weight. The plane was a mighty beast and its awe-inspiring strength buzzed through every one of his five senses. The plane was also a wicked scalpel, capable of incredible accuracy.

He looked through the head-up display of electronic words and symbols to the scenery beyond. Sighting a ridgeline, Eli pointed the plane's nose toward it. He placed the green velocity vector circle directly over the point above the ridgeline where he aimed to pass. It was seven miles away, but traveling at this speed, the F-22 would cut through that exact airspace in one minute flat.

Last night, Penelope had told him her three concerns about him. He was glad she had, because now he knew what the obstacles were.

He'd faced obstacles before. When he'd been determined to get into the Academy. When he'd been determined to become a pilot. Every single day on the job.

He was a professional at facing challenges.

His plane rocketed forward, the adrenaline in his blood stream making him feel sharply, wholly alive.

* * *

In her rented kitchen space, Penelope stirred glazed peaches and swayed to the melody of "Sweet Child O' Mine."

She served five types of pie year-round. Peach, pecan, apple, mixed berry, and chocolate (Theo's Pie). Plus, she always offered one or two seasonal pies, such as cherry or pumpkin, depending on which ingredients were fresh. Each pie was available as a whole pie or by the slice and each slice could be ordered plain or à la mode.

She kept her drink offerings simple. Water, hot coffee, and hot tea in the cold months. Water, milk, iced coffee, and iced tea in the hot months.

Today's seasonal pies, strawberry and key lime, had just come out of the commercial ovens opposite her humongous central workspace. The three peach pies she was assembling now were the last of today's efforts.

She'd steeled herself against Eli yesterday, leaving the instant she'd finished her fried chicken dinner. She wished she'd been as successful at steeling herself against thoughts of him. Instead, she'd been replaying and replaying memories of the things he'd said to her last night. Each time she did, emotional glitter spun in her chest, glittering.

His words had been powerful enough but the *way that he'd said them!* He'd spoken in that unvarnished way he had, looking directly at her. His hair had been rumpled and she'd been repeatedly distracted by the play of tendons in his masculine forearms.

The hurt she harbored toward him was behaving like a chunk of arctic ice. Pieces of it kept cracking off and toppling into the ocean. Problem was, she understood that the strength of her own desires could wreck her objectivity and persuade her to fall into a relationship with Eli even if doing so was seriously ill-advised.

She slid the peach pies into the oven, cleaned her workspace, then decided to treat herself to pie. She did a great deal of tasting but didn't usually indulge in a full slice at 10:02 a.m. This morning, though, it felt imperative. Pie would lift her spirits.

She plated a wedge of key lime and took slow bites. Critically, she assessed its balance and flavor. The creamy tartness of the lime provided an ideal complement to the crisp, buttery richness of the graham cracker crust.

This pie was exactly as she wanted it to be.

She only wished that relationships were as simple as pie.

• • •

It was Taco Tuesday at Pablo's, a casual roadside joint north of town. The place smelled like fried tortillas and sounded like mariachi music.

Eli and his friend Sam Turner had just given their server their order. They handed her their menus, but instead of leaving, the young woman shot Eli a long and hopeful look before giving the same to Sam. "Your accent's great," she told Sam.

"Where are you from?"

"Australia."

Her eyes widened with awe. "Wow."

Eli relaxed back in his seat, watching with amusement as she asked Sam follow-up questions.

He'd met Sam at the gym shortly after moving to Misty River. He, Sam, Theo, and several others played basketball together at least once a week. Eli had hung out with Sam enough to know that women almost always flirted with him and people of every age and gender asked him about his accent. It was unusual to run across an Australian accent in the North Georgia mountains.

What Eli could predict with ninety-five percent certainty: their server's interest in Sam would get her nowhere.

Eli sensed a knot of grief at Sam's core and suspected that a woman might be to blame but didn't know for sure. Sam was disciplined, hard-working, and solemn. He lived alone on a historic farm outside town and utilized much of what he grew at his farm-to-table restaurant.

Their server moved off.

"I could use your help with something," Eli said.

"Yeah?" Sam dipped a chip in the salsa bowl.

"You know how I feel about Penelope Quinn,

right?"

Sam surveyed him with pale green eyes. "I knew how you felt about her before you left. You still feel the same way?"

"I feel even more strongly now." Two days had passed since his dinner with Penelope. Eli had told Theo he was free to babysit in the evenings during the work week, but so far, Theo hadn't taken him up on his offer. Penelope or Aubrey's friends or members of Theo's church had been covering shifts with Madeline whenever the baby wasn't with her parents. "When I saw her a couple of days ago, she listed the things about me that concern her."

"Huh." Sam dipped another chip.

"I need to show her that she can count on me to be truthful. That I'm not too macho to communicate my feelings. And that I'm not afraid to make a fool of myself for love."

"Is that all?" Sam asked dryly.

"Do you have any ideas for me?"

"None. I'm terrible at relationships."

"Help me brainstorm. How can I show her I'm truthful?"

"Tell her you think she's gained weight?" Humor creased Sam's expression.

Eli chuckled. "You really are terrible at relationships."

"Told you."

"Other ideas?"

"Tell her you don't like how that guy who works for her always keeps talking after a conversation's over," Sam said. "Or tell her that her chocolate pie needs a touch more salt."

"There's no way I'm going to criticize her weight, her employee, or her pie."

"I thought you wanted to be truthful."

"But not critical."

"How come she's worried about your truthfulness? Have you lied to her about something in the past?"

"By remaining silent about something important, yes."

"Then don't make the same mistake. Talk to her about the thing you didn't talk to her about the last time."

Sam was right. Of course Sam was right. But, *shoot*. If he told her what he knew about his squadron's future, that would put him in a position that sucked. "What about communicating my feelings? Let's brainstorm that."

"Write her a poem?"

"I don't read or write poetry."

"Which is why she'll like it when you make the effort to write a poem for her."

Eli regarded Sam doubtfully. "What if I write her a letter?"

"Sure. Or a song?"

"I could hang a banner above her apartment door."

"You're a pilot. Say 'I love you' through sky-writing."

Their server returned to top off their drinks. She gave them both a flashing smile. They resumed their conversation when she'd gone.

"She also wants me to show her that I'm willing to make a fool of myself for love." Eli scratched the back of his head. "How do I do that?"

"Rent a hot air balloon and land it in front of her house?"

"I could buy up a whole day's worth of pie from her, then give it away free to celebrate Penelope Day."

"Get a megaphone and walk around talking about how great she is?"

"I could serenade her from the sidewalk."

Sam shrugged. "All of those things will definitely result in you making a fool of yourself."

He tried to imagine himself walking around Misty River with a megaphone. "If I, ah, need your help with any of these, you'd be willing, right?"

"Definitely not."

"By *definitely not* do you mean yes?"

"Definitely not."

●　●　●

Across town, Penelope and Cameron were on a date.

Penelope lined up the putter they'd given her at the Putt Putt golf counter. She swung carefully and connected with her magenta-colored ball. It rolled just past the hole and continued going until it plunked against the concrete lip.

"Sorry about that," Cameron said.

He kept apologizing every time she missed. He didn't seem to comprehend that she was not competitively invested in this game.

"Should I go?" he asked. He was a stickler for the rules. "I'm farthest from the hole, so I think it's me."

"Be my guest." She stood her putter upright like a cane and crossed one foot over the other.

Cameron took a great deal of time checking his line and strategizing. Bless him.

He had very thick black hair and a strong, stocky body. He looked like he could be a mobster's favorite son. But his personality belonged to a Kindergarten Sunday School teacher. Uncertain, earnest, squeaky clean.

The sun had almost finished draining color from the sky. A nearby light post lit Cameron's pale blue button-down and beige pants. In the drone of the fake waterfall beside her, her thoughts wandered to a winter night and a secret dance and a stolen kiss—

"Penelope?"

She straightened, returning to the present. He'd sunk his shot. She putted. Missed.

"Sorry," he said.

The next time, her ball finally went in.

Cameron made a dutiful notation on the score card using a miniature pencil. "Do you want to go on to the next hole? Or we could sit a while?" He indicated the indentation carved into a large imitation stone to create a bench.

"Let's go on to the next hole."

"Cool." He gave her a besotted smile.

They arrived at hole nine, where it appeared the aim was to hit into a rectangular opening beneath a windmill.

"Would you like to go first?" he asked. "Technically, I should since I had the lowest score on the last hole."

"You go."

When it was her turn, her ball obediently sailed

into the opening.

"Awesome!"

"Thanks, Cameron." They progressed down to the circle of green where their balls had emerged.

"You're farthest out," he said.

He had so many good qualities. Cameron was brainy. Employed. He had straight white teeth. He did not live with his parents. Like her, he loved Legos and Jesus. Best of all, he was not in the Air Force.

But this would have to be their last date.

She was not enamored with the prospect of spending her days answering his questions. *Would you like to open the door or should I, Penelope? Is it okay if I go to work now? May I lock the car? Can I get myself a drink?*

Cameron didn't have a Montana heritage or quick comebacks. He didn't know that she liked fried chicken and he didn't babysit his friend's newborn baby and he didn't make her laugh.

His name was not Eli.

Chapter Six

Penelope was spending the Fourth of July inside the 1955 Jewel camper trailer that she'd gutted and converted into a mobile pie shop. From her position at the window where customers placed orders, she had a view of the town's central park. The old brick buildings framing the park contained a cute mix of shops, government offices, restaurants, and corporate spaces.

Every time the stress of the busy day had begun to fray her nerves, she'd lifted her gaze to the ancient, calming mountains in the distance.

Geologists speculated that the Blue Ridge Mountains had once resembled their young cousin, the Rocky Mountains—all jagged and high and self-important with youth. But the centuries had worn the range down in the same way that time wears down and matures all things. Because of that, the slopes, hollows, and aged forests of the Blue Ridge whispered to Penelope of their stalwart ability to endure and endure and *endure*.

Misty River had been founded in 1823. Like a child hesitant to stray too far from its mother, the town's earliest buildings clung close to the river. Misty River's hills wore forests that turned brilliant with color every autumn. Waterfalls carved pools into the earth. Mist often hovered low here. And clouds often hovered high.

Through the decades, the residents of this town had stitched a tapestry marked with shades of honor as well as shame.

When gold had been found in these mountains in 1829, European and American settlers flocked to the area and, in doing so, trespassed on the ancestral land of the Cherokee. The Cherokee fought for their rights in court. The government bowed to pressure from miners and corporations, eventually forcing the migration of the Native Americans via the Trail of Tears.

Later, when America hovered on the brink of Civil War, Rabun County voted not to secede from the union. They were overruled by urban centers. Georgia, and with it Misty River, had gone to war for the Confederacy and thus for the continuance of the abomination of slavery.

During World War I, a hero from Misty River gave his life to protect his fellow soldiers at the

Battle of Cantigny and was honored with the Distinguished Service Cross.

In World War II, a nurse from Misty River had valiantly treated soldiers in Normandy after D-Day.

Penelope's town had emerged from its pockmarked past humbled, wiser, and with a patriotic heart. It was famous for its beauty, its orchards, its vineyards, and a group of kids (now adults) known as the Miracle Five.

Ever since today's Fourth of July parade and the ceremony honoring servicemen and women had concluded, throngs of people had been drifting to the classic car show nearby, the carnival rides at First Baptist Church, and Polka-Dot Apron Pies.

It was three thirty in the afternoon now and the onslaught had finally calmed. Blowing a tendril of hair out of her eye, Penelope smiled at the next customer in line, a cute little grandmother.

"Two slices of apple pie à la mode," the older woman said.

"You bet. Anything to drink?"

"Just water, please."

"Certainly." Penelope passed the order along to her sole employee, Kevin.

Turquoise paint coated the outside of her trailer. Pink-and-white-striped wallpaper brightened the inside. Two windows crowned with awnings—one for ordering, one for pie pick-up—marked the exterior.

Penelope handed the grandmother her change.

Whenever she and Kevin worked the camper at the same time, like today, she ran the register and he plated. She had an easier rapport with customers and Kevin was fastidious at plating.

She passed over the two slices of pie, crowned with scoops of photo-worthy vanilla ice cream softening in cinnamony rivulets down the pie's sides thanks to the day's eighty-seven-degree temperature.

She glanced across at Kevin. "How's our inventory?" It would be a travesty to run out of apple pie on America's birthday.

"Running lowest on apple, but we'll have more than enough to make it to the end of the day. Good planning, boss."

"Thanks."

A recent college graduate, Kevin was pale, slight, and already prematurely balding.

"Really good planning, boss." Kevin nodded at her, retaining hopeful eye contact.

"Thanks again."

"Yes, ma'am. I'm impressed."

She turned to take the next customer's order.

"You made just enough." Kevin was still holding up his end of their chat, despite that she'd moved on to a new conversation. She could feel his gaze on her.

"You really have a knack for calculating how much we'll sell—"

She interrupted Kevin kindly. "One pecan, please."

Glancing up to take the next customer's order, she spotted . . .

Eli.

Eli.

Her heart executed a surprised somersault. It had been months upon months since she'd glanced up from her food truck window and seen him standing in her line. It was a Wednesday. But, of course, he was off work for the holiday.

Belatedly, she realized she'd completely missed the order the family of four had just placed.

"Sorry!" she told the mom. "Can you repeat that one more time, please?"

After inputting their order on the iPad and flipping the screen toward the mom to sign, she shot a surreptitious glance at Eli. He'd come alone, wearing a T-shirt that read *USAF*. She loved the fit of the jeans he'd chosen and his metal-rimmed sunglasses.

The two young women ahead of Eli in line kept sliding peeks at him. She'd spent enough time with Eli to have noticed that the admiration of women followed him wherever he went. This time, however, the interest of the women didn't sit well with her. At all.

Penelope passed the family of four their pie order.

The black-haired woman standing in front of Eli struck up a conversation with him. Penelope wrinkled her nose, straining to hear what they were saying, but couldn't quite make it out. Eli would answer politely, of that she was certain.

The black-haired woman gesticulated with her hands, laughed.

Eli smiled in return, his attention flicking up to Penelope just as he did so. Which tempted Penelope to suspect that his smile was for her.

Eventually, he reached the front of the line.

"Hi." Not her best verbal opener.

"Hi."

"Would you care for some pie?"

"Please."

"The usual?"

"Yeah."

"I'll bring it around." She motioned with her head to the camper's side.

"How much do I owe you?"

You owe me about a million apology notes for making me dream of you for the past three nights in a row. "This is my treat."

She turned to Kevin. "One peach à la mode, please. And if you think you can man the fort, I'm going to take a break." It might be smart, or it might be dumb, but she wanted some time with Eli.

"Sure, boss."

She removed her yellow polka-dot apron. "I'll be back in thirty minutes or so."

"Happy to man the fort." He handed her the slice of peach pie. "You can count on me." He didn't look away.

"I'll be leaving now."

"This is a great time for you to go. It's not as busy as it was." He gave her a pleasant look of expectation, as if waiting for her to say something more.

"Kevin, customers are waiting to place their order."

"Ah!" He stepped toward the window. "I love all the patriotic clothing. It's encouraging to see—"

She escaped out the door. Meeting Eli at the camper's end, she handed him his pie. "Fancy seeing you here. Were you hungry for pie?"

"Always. But I came to see you."

She got lost in his soft brown eyes. *Gah!* "Better get started on that." She nudged her chin toward his pie. "As you know, I take it as a personal insult when people don't eat it right away and let the ice cream turn into plain old cream."

He lowered his vision to his dessert and released a sound of appreciation at the sight of its golden-brown flaky crust and filling of glistening peaches. He picked up his biodegradable spork. "What about you? Are you hungry or thirsty? If you can get away for a minute, I'll buy you food."

"I am hungry, and I can get away for a minute, but I'll buy my own food."

"I'm buying," he said, unperturbed.

"That's not necessary—"

He lifted his pie plate. "You just gave me pie. Did you notice how graciously I accepted it, without arguing?"

She smiled. "Fine. Rumor has it that your friend Sam's selling sliders over at Sugar Maple Kitchen. You can buy me a few of those."

Side by side they ambled down streets closed to traffic.

Ten years ago, *Travel + Leisure* had done a spread on Misty River, declaring it a hidden gem. Afterward, the town had become a not-so-hidden gem. The influx of tourists had brought an answering wave of businesses that had filled every previously empty retail space downtown. Almost all of those businesses had raised pop-up tents outside today, where they were selling their specialties, distributing freebies, or passing out flyers.

"Your pie is even better than I remembered," Eli said, glancing at her.

"Thank you." He'd always been an avid supporter of her business.

A family wearing matching flag T-shirts from Old Navy passed going the other direction. A girl with long pigtails holding an assortment of navy, white, and gold balloons ran down the street in front of them.

"You must've been in a good mood this morning," Eli observed.

Her momentary confusion gave way to clarity. "Did you come to that conclusion based on my shoes?"

He made a sound of assent.

"Your deduction's correct."

Her parents and Theo and Lila and her other friends all knew that she was extremely loyal to her Vans and that she had enough of them that she could go two weeks straight without repeating a pair. But no one except Eli had noticed that she chose her Vans based on her state of mind. And then chose her outfit based on her Vans. This morning, she'd selected a red pair, then matched them with a white tee under overall shorts.

She tipped her knock-off Cartier sunglasses from her casual up-do down over her eyes. Designer sunglass styles appealed to her, but she only bought knock-offs because she was the owner of a pie shop, not a Swiss bank.

A green tent shaded the serving table Sam had set up in front of Sugar Maple Kitchen. He stood before a small barbecue that was releasing curls of beef-scented smoke.

To her way of thinking, Sam was a genius with food. His dishes were an inspiration to her—creative, healthy, fresh, and blow-your-mind tasty. He'd moved to Misty River four years ago and she still vividly recalled the very first item she'd purchased at his restaurant, a Paleo cinnamon roll. It had been a revelation to her and, when she'd polished it off, she'd sought Sam out and introduced herself. He was so talented that talking to him made her feel the same way she felt when talking to her pastor, slightly self-conscious and dazzled.

Eli and Sam exchanged greetings, then Penelope

requested two sliders and a glass of iced tea. Eli pulled out his wallet and peeled off bills, which he passed to the female employee of The Kitchen manning the cash box.

Eli winked happily at Penelope.

She rolled her eyes. If it delighted him to pay, fine. This was *not* a date. This was him showing up at her pie shop. And her hanging out with him during a work break.

Sam flipped her slider patties on the grill. Tall and strapping, with olive skin and brown hair, he was the embodiment of what every American woman imagined the ideal Aussie man should look like. Yet Sam didn't come with the classic happy-go-lucky, easy-to-laugh, quick-to-throw-back-a-beer Aussie personality. He was closed-off some-how. Wounded, maybe.

Sam represented the trifecta of dating eligibility to the women in this town. He was 1) Respectable, 2) Handsome, and 3) Foreign. Several of her friends had crushes on Sam, yet he hadn't asked any of them out, which had led to collective confusion and misery.

"Eli told me that Theo's wife's been in the hos-pital," Sam said to Penelope. "How is she?"

"Much better," Penelope answered. "She's been steadily improving. So much so, the doctors are going to release her from the hospital today."

"Beaut," Sam said in his charming accent.

"She'll need to continue taking medications and she'll need to go in for appointments pretty often." She pushed her sunglasses up her nose. "But they're confident that she'll regain full health."

"Who's keeping Madeline today?" Eli asked.

"A few of Aubrey's friends."

"Are they still going to need help with Madeline after they're home?" Eli asked.

"Yes. Aubrey's not strong enough to take care of Madeline by herself yet and Theo really needs to catch up on work. Several of us are going to take turns at the house when Theo's not there, so Aubrey can rest."

"I can help weeknights and weekends," Eli said.

"I'll bring food by for them," Sam offered.

"That's fabulously kind. Thank you."

Sam moved Penelope's sliders onto buns and went to work adding garnishes.

"Sam and I ate at Pablo's last night," Eli told her.

"We had the most ridiculous conversation I've ever had," Sam said.

"Then we went out to Sam's farm and I tried to talk him into watching the Rockies game."

"Eli's interest in watching baseball on TV is one of his flaws," Sam said.

"Baseball's cool," she said.

"Baseball's awful," Sam stated.

"Don't waste your breath trying to convince him that it's not," Eli said to her. "We ended up watching Aussie Rules Football."

"Best sport in the world," Sam said.

"He calls it footy." Eli lifted his brows.

"Is it like American football?" she asked.

"Better," Sam answered. "There's not so much starting and stopping."

"It's what would happen if soccer and rugby had a baby," Eli said, then headed toward the trash can a few storefronts down, doubtless so he could throw away his empty pie plate.

"Eli's a good guy," Sam said to her when Eli was out of earshot.

"Yeah. He is."

He glanced up from her sliders, meeting her eyes. "Are you going to go out with him?"

"I think I might be dooming myself to heart-break if I do."

"Or opening yourself up to happiness." He handed her the plate of food. Eli carried her tea and Penelope shot Sam a grateful wave as they parted.

"Still starstruck by Sam, I see," Eli said.

"Yep," she replied fervently.

They found a sidewalk bench in the shade and she started in on the sliders. *Delicious.*

Companionable quiet settled over them as they watched people flow past.

Inwardly, Eli argued with himself. Penelope wouldn't date him until he was honest with her, but as soon as he was honest with her, she wouldn't want to date him.

She looked incredibly cute today, with her hair piled on top of her head. Her long legs were bare and toned. And she smelled like pie.

He didn't want to push her away. Yet in order to win her over, the first obstacle he had to overcome was her belief that she couldn't count on him to be honest. And, frankly, if he couldn't be honest with her even when he didn't want to be, he didn't deserve to date her.

"I learned on Monday that I'll be restationed to Germany in January," he said.

His words appeared to catch her unprepared—like a thief sneaking into a house. Her face went blank as she turned to him. "Restationing means that you're being sent there permanently?"

"Semi-permanently. I'll be sent somewhere else

after a few years there."

He thought he saw a flare of sadness in her features. "How do you feel about the news?" she asked.

"Not great."

"Germany's beautiful."

"Germany comes with language differences, cultural differences, and climate differences."

"Yes, but think about all the places you'll get to see."

"Right, but you live here. I don't love the idea of moving far away from you."

She went still.

"I'm afraid that, because I'm going, I won't be able to convince you to give me a shot."

"I'm glad you told me that you're going, Eli. I appreciate it. I do."

A vague answer. She had not responded by assuring him that he *did* still have a shot. His mood darkened at the edges like paper held to a candle flame. He'd done what he'd failed to do the last time. He'd told her about an upcoming assignment as soon as he'd found out. He should find comfort in that. But didn't.

They talked about other things while she polished off the food, then they visited a few different shops. She purchased a bar of handmade soap, a fake USA tattoo for her cheek, and a pottery fruit bowl.

On the way back to the pie truck, they passed a nondescript corridor between buildings. He gestured to it and asked her, "Do you remember?" Their kiss had occurred just yards from where they were standing.

"I do."

He walked into the corridor.

She hesitated. He kept walking, hoping she'd trail behind him. She did.

The passage opened into the small courtyard. On its far side, the river. The town bank and post office wrapped around its other sides. It had been deserted the night they'd kissed. Then, the sky had been a blanket of stars and red and white flowers had filled the planting beds. It was deserted again now, the bank and post office both closed. The sky shone bright blue. The planting beds overflowed with pink flowers.

This was the first time he'd returned here since that night, which caused memories from the past to hurtle forward.

He'd been carrying her packages. He set them down carefully. "I think I reached for your hand, like this." He extended his arm. "May I have this dance?"

For a long moment, she didn't move. "A few days ago, my answer would have been no." She set her hand in his.

"But then I calmed your niece's crying fit."

"And bought me sliders."

"I knew those sliders were a good investment."

Wordlessly, they two-stepped around the courtyard. No music this time, just the distant sound of the crowds, birdsong, and the hum of the river pouring over rock.

He twirled her and she spun beneath their joined hands. She came up against him, her palms against the fabric of his T-shirt. His profile was just a few inches from hers. Her body felt feminine and lean in his arms.

Heat rushed through his bloodstream. His breath came fast and uneven.

At this point, they'd kissed the last time. He simply stared at her this time, waiting to see what she'd choose. What she wanted.

He saw desire and conflict and worry in her.

He willed her to care about him more than she cared about her rule or the fact that he'd be gone in January—

She stepped back, breaking the contact between them.

He held himself still.

"Thanks for the sliders and tea!" she said. "Good day to you."

Then she lifted her packages and hurried down the corridor. He watched her go, unsure whether she was fleeing from him, the pleasure he offered, or the pain that would come as part of the bargain.

Chapter Seven

Herding cats had to be easier than coaching second grade boys' basketball.

On the evening of July fifth, Eli led the Sharpshooters' practice. He ran drills, taught, ran drills, taught, then finished with a scrimmage. Several times, he stopped their scrimmage to explain or act out a visual example he wanted them to follow.

"Okay, guys," Eli said when they had just five minutes of time left. "Grab a drink, then bring it in." The boys, red-faced and sweaty, located their water bottles and plopped onto the court's floor in front of him.

Creighton, who'd spent the practice sitting on the sidelines swiping and punching his phone's screen, had informed Eli earlier that the next team they were playing also had zero wins. This meant Monday night's game was the best chance they'd have all season of coming out on top.

"I know you guys usually get to the games fifteen minutes early, but I'm going to send out an email to your parents, asking them to bring you to the game on Monday twenty minutes early because I have a surprise to give you."

That caught their attention.

"What is it?" the shortest kid asked.

"You'll have to get there twenty minutes early to find out. So. What two things did we work on the most at practice today?"

"Pooping and farting," the class clown answered with a snicker.

Eli pretended he hadn't heard.

"Defense," one boy said.

"Rebounding," another offered.

"Yes."

Creighton appeared at Eli's side. He clapped three times. "Hustle out there, guys. *Hustle!*"

"Does Coach Theo ever bribe these kids?" Eli asked Creighton.

Creighton lifted his brows and gave a small shake of his head.

"That's probably because Coach Theo doesn't think you're old enough for bribery," Eli said to the team. "But I do."

"What's bribery?" the least-coordinated boy asked.

"It's when you offer to give something to

someone if they'll do what you want in exchange. I'm guessing that parents frown on bribery. But lucky for you guys, I'm not a parent."

Their small faces sharpened with interest.

"We're playing the Bricklayers on Monday night and we're going to bring a full court press defense. We're also going to rebound. When we have the ball, we'll take our time and attempt smart shots. If you steal the ball from the other team or if you rebound a ball, Coach Creighton here is going to add a tiger claw tattoo to your arm the next time you sit on the bench."

"A permanent tattoo?" a red-haired kid asked.

That's right. We're going to ink a permanent tattoo onto your arm on the sidelines of a youth basketball game. "A temporary tattoo. At the end of the game, you'll count up your tiger claws and we'll see who has the most."

"So what are you bribing us with?" Redhead again. His mouth twisted with confusion.

"The tattoos. If you do what I want—steal the ball or rebound the ball—I'll give you a tattoo. Deal?"

"Deal," they said in unison.

• • •

Penelope immersed herself in a bath composed half

of water and half of thick, glossy, vanilla-scented bubbles. Her fingers drifted back and forth, creating fanciful patterns in the suds.

Everyone stationed at Ricker Air Force Base left eventually.

Her years in Misty River had taught her this truth very, very well. She didn't date airmen in part *because* they left. So why had the realization that Eli would be leaving caused a wrench of pain so deep within that she still hadn't recovered from it?

The town, their social circle, Theo, herself. None would be the same without his distinctive presence.

Roy's flat face appeared over the lip of the tub. His attention ticked from bubble to bubble until he finally started batting at them with a paw.

Yesterday, when she and Eli had danced, she'd once again been confronted with her enormous longing for him. Her whole body had been *aching* to kiss him. Yet her deep emotions concerning him were at war with one another. She hadn't forgotten Lila's tears. Michelle's tears. Destiny's tears. The pain Eli himself had caused her the one time she'd risked kissing him. The fact that he'd be just as gone, come January, as all the other airmen who'd come before him.

She'd told Sam that she did not want to doom

herself to heartbreak. And a truer statement had never been given.

With Eli, falling in love felt like the easiest option in the world. It would take no effort to fall. He was brave, selfless, impressive, funny, smart, and inexplicably dedicated to her.

Heartbreak was the thing that would take effort. If things didn't work out with Eli, she'd be left with a canyon of sorrow to scale.

●　●　●

Eli pulled down the top few inches of his flight suit zipper on Friday as he strode away from his aircraft across the tarmac. He clasped his helmet bag in one hand and used his other to rake his sweat-drenched hair into place. Now that the aircraft were parked safely in their shelters, the shrill noise of their jet engines was fading quickly. The Raptors that had been so dynamic minutes before now looked dormant, the smell of burnt fuel the only symbol of the power they'd just displayed.

Inside the squadron lounge he pushed two pieces of bread into the toaster, ate a banana, took a long drink of water, poured himself coffee, then waited for Shooter to finish with the butter and butter knife. The other pilots were all talking and jostling in the small space, trying to grab food and a drink during the few minutes they had to spare before the debrief.

They'd just completed an air-to-air mission. Half of them had been designated good guys. Half of them bad guys. They'd all had to operate under the assigned parameters, make split-second decisions, and fly with precision.

Their cockpit displays had been recorded throughout the exercise and they were about to review the tapes, which meant each pilot's mistakes and successes would be shown to all.

Eli would find out if he'd won the war or lost it. They'd eventually agree on learning points, but until then he could count on the debrief to be tense and hard-hitting. No matter how senior you were, if you'd screwed up during the mission, even the junior pilots would call you out.

He didn't think he'd screwed up. He was a perfectionist when it came to flying and he expected to be told during the debrief that he'd done well.

Even so, this was not the time to think about poetry.

He placed his toast on a paper plate and buttered it while thinking about poetry.

The next obstacle in the path to winning Penelope's heart? Show her he could communicate his feelings.

He'd decided to write her a poem.

Looking for inspiration, he'd studied "High Flight" by John Gillespie Magee Jr., a favorite poem of aviators. He'd read stuff by Shakespeare, Browning, and Byron.

He'd started a dozen poems and ended up throwing them all in the trash because he didn't think *Your hair is like a cirrocumulus cloud* or *I like you more than pulling nine Gs* was going to do the trick.

"Do you know anything about poetry?" he asked Skid.

She swallowed a mouthful of power bar, eyebrows lifting. "A little. Why?"

"I'm trying to write a poem."

She grinned. Her frizzy blond hair always looked angry to be trapped into the low ponytail she wore on the job. "Why?"

"Because I think Penelope might like it."

"There's nothing you could do to make Penelope like you," she teased.

"That's really helpful, thanks."

"I'd advise you to keep it simple and honest," she said.

"Rhyming? Not rhyming?"

"It doesn't matter. What matters is that you break open that lump of coal you call a heart and force it to express itself."

"Okay, but what style of poem should I write? How long should it be?"

"If I give you more help, Penelope won't be moved because she'll know it didn't come from you."

He scowled.

"I wouldn't stress about it too much," she said as she walked toward the debriefing room. "All your efforts are going to fail, Big Sky. That woman is out of your league."

● ● ●

"What are you smiling about?" Aubrey asked Penelope on Sunday.

"Am I smiling?"

"It was subtle, but yes. You had a dreamy kind of smile on your face."

"I'm just glad that you're home and doing so well."

"Aww." Aubrey sat on the floor of her living room next to one of those baby gym thingama-bobs. Madeline lay beneath the arching bars and dangling toys on a blanket, looking upward with an expression Penelope translated as polite confusion.

While it was certainly true that she was glad Aubrey was home and doing so well, her smile had sprung from a different source entirely. She'd been looking at the text Eli had sent her yesterday.

I know you're not interested in going out on a date. But would you be willing to share your weekend schedule with me? That way, I can run into you coincidentally. I have something I'd like to give you.

The text had given her a swoony thrill when she'd first seen it. Since then, she'd viewed it several more times because it continued to deliver on thrills.

She'd debated how to respond. Eventually, she and Eli would see each other at a social gathering. He could give her whatever he had to give her then.

Only, he'd sparked her curiosity. And as ill-advised as it might be, she didn't want to wait for a social occasion to see him again. She'd texted back, *I'll be at my apartment for a few hours on Sunday afternoon, starting at 3:00. You can run into me coincidentally then.*

Theo had taken time off for Madeline's birth and then again for Aubrey's more recent hospitalization. He'd been working from home as much as possible the past few days, but he still had a lot of business to catch up on at the office. Penelope and the rest of Aubrey's circle had been lending a hand whenever Theo was away. Aubrey was growing stronger by the day. Soon she wouldn't need backup.

Penelope had gone to church this morning and come here after. She expected Theo to arrive home soon to relieve her, which would give her time to straighten her apartment and her hair before Eli's visit.

Picking up the *European Pies* cookbook she'd brought with her, she made herself comfortable on the sofa and started to read.

Aubrey levered herself to standing, then reached down to scoop up the infant. "Madeline's getting sleepy. I'm going to go tuck her in."

"You bet. Call if you need my help with anything."

"I will."

She eyed a recipe for Swedish apple pie. How did one say *yummy* in Swedish? She looked it up on her phone. *Smaskigt.* This pie looked *smaskigt.*

The sound of Madeline's irritable crying reached her. She let it go on for a few minutes, mindful of the fact that poor Aubrey hadn't had one square second alone in her house with her child in days. If Penelope were in Aubrey's position, she wouldn't want well-meaning people rushing to her side every time Madeline squawked.

"Anything I can do?" Penelope finally called.

"Thanks," Aubrey called back, "but I think she's settling down now."

Sure enough, the fussing gradually gave way to the strains of the lullaby music Aubrey played on a portable speaker.

Penelope considered a German cottage cheese pie. It looked—she consulted her phone—*lecker*. Then an Irish banoffee pie, made with bananas, caramel, and cream. Apparently the Irish word *sobhlasta* meant delicious. "Sobhlasta," Penelope whispered in her best (not good) Irish accent.

It might be fun to spend a few weeks this fall selling European pies at her shop. She could decorate the truck with European trappings. Market her European pies around town . . .

Penelope looked up from the cookbook, listening. The house was unusually still. She could hear the lullaby sounds and nothing else.

"Aubrey?" Penelope called. She wanted to be respectful of her privacy. But she also needed to be attentive.

No answer.

Unease slipped around her eerily . . . like an eel

sliding against her skin in murky water.

She stood. She'd just go check to see if Aubrey was napping. As she rounded the turn in the hallway that led to the bedrooms, she saw Aubrey, lying on her back on the floor outside the nursery.

Fear drove the air from Penelope's lungs. She fell to her knees beside her sister-in-law. "Aubrey? Are you okay?" She gently shook her shoulder.

Aubrey was not okay, nor awake. She could feel the warmth of Aubrey's skin through her lightweight summer top. She was breathing as if asleep, but . . . Penelope gave her a slightly harder shake. Aubrey wasn't sleeping. She wouldn't have taken a nap in the middle of her hallway floor. She was unconscious.

Penelope punched 911 into her phone with trembling fingers.

You're the Rock of Gibraltar! This is not the time to fall apart.

And so she wouldn't.

A female voice answered.

"My sister-in-law was—was diagnosed with a pulmonary embolism just over a week ago." Her words emerged shaky but quick. "She's currently unconscious. I need an ambulance here immediately." She rattled off the address and the woman told her that an ambulance was on its way.

99

The dispatcher kept Penelope on the line, asking questions about Aubrey that Penelope answered as she went in search of Madeline.

Horror clawed its way upward, past her tightening throat. Where was the baby?

Penelope was on duty. The one in charge of making sure Aubrey and Madeline were safe and well. She'd screwed up.

She checked Madeline's nursery first. Little piles of clean baby clothing sat on the rug, but Madeline was not asleep in the crib.

The woman on the other end of the line was attempting to ask more questions, but all Penelope could think was *where's Madeline?*

She checked the bathroom next to the nursery. Not here.

She slid to a halt in Theo and Aubrey's bedroom. Madeline was swaddled and clicked into her baby swing. The apparatus swished back and forth languidly in a pool of sunlight, its sound masked by the music.

Madeline was fine, thank God.

"Ma'am?" the dispatcher said.

"I'm here." She dashed back to Aubrey's side and followed the woman's instructions. She raised Aubrey's legs a foot off the ground to promote blood flow to her head. She looked to see if

Aubrey was wearing any restrictive clothing that needed loosening (she wasn't), then checked for an airway obstruction (also negative).

"Does she appear to have injured herself in the fall?" the woman asked.

"No."

Aubrey began to stir.

"Aubrey?"

Her sister-in-law frowned and cracked open her eyes.

"She's waking up," Penelope told the dispatcher.

"Good, good," the woman replied.

"Can you hear me?" Penelope asked. She must look bizarre, kneeling on the hallway floor, holding both of Aubrey's legs in the air.

"Yes. Did I . . . pass out?"

"I think so, yes."

Worry creased Aubrey's face. "Madeline?"

"She's absolutely fine. Still sleeping in her baby swing."

"I'd just finished folding her clothes." Aubrey motioned toward the nursery. "I stood up quickly and it made me dizzy. I stopped moving, but it just seemed to get worse and so I sat down . . . here. I was about to call you, but then sound and light just sort of . . . left me."

"An ambulance is coming."

"I'm not sure I need an ambulance. I'm feeling . . . fairly okay." She pressed a hand to her forehead. "I think you can put my legs down."

"Can I put her legs down?" she asked the dispatcher.

"That should be fine, just do so slowly and carefully."

Penelope did as the woman had directed.

Aubrey tried to push herself into a seated position—

"Would you do me a favor and remain lying down until the paramedics get here?" she asked Aubrey.

Her sister-in-law gave a slight nod.

The sound of an ambulance siren reached her, faint but rapidly increasing in volume. Penelope thanked the dispatcher and disconnected the call.

"I'm so sorry that I let this happen on my watch." Guilt had turned Penelope's stomach into a ball of nausea. "This is my fault."

"This is *not* your fault," Aubrey said. "How much time has passed since you heard Madeline crying?"

"Fifteen minutes at most."

"After she calmed down, I kept rocking her for five minutes. Then folded clothes for several more minutes. Which means I could only have been out for a couple of minutes. You must have found me immediately."

Penelope let the paramedics inside, explaining the situation as she led them to Aubrey.

The man and woman immediately took over, calm and confident. Penelope leaned against the hallway wall, hovering out of their way and chewing on her thumbnail.

They concluded that Aubrey had simply suffered a fainting spell. According to the paramedics, the blood-thinning medication she was on for her blood clot could cause dizziness. Unfortunately, the medication could also cause internal bleeding if the person taking it fell, as Aubrey had. It sounded like she'd been sitting down when she'd fainted, so hopefully, she hadn't fallen far. Internal bleeding was a serious thing, and so back to the hospital Aubrey was going in the ambulance.

"You'll call Theo for me?" Aubrey asked Penelope. As always in times of crisis, Aubrey became almost preternaturally calm.

"Of course."

"And take care of Madeline?"

"Yes."

"Thank you."

The paramedics swept her from the house.

Penelope stood at the living room's front window, watching as they secured Aubrey in the ambulance, then pulled away from the curb. Next, she made her way to Madeline's side. Her niece, wrapped in swaddling and peaceful music, had slept straight through the commotion.

She pulled out her phone. Trying not to cry, she dialed her brother.

Chapter Eight

Penelope had stood him up.

When she hadn't answered his knock a few minutes before three, he'd figured she must be on her way.

Then 3:00 had arrived. 3:05.

His optimism had drained as his watch had counted the minutes to 3:15. He'd texted her and received no response.

It was now 3:30 and he needed to face the fact that she wasn't coming. Her message was clear. She didn't want him.

Loneliness crept up from the floorboards and invaded his body. He felt it inside him, heavy and empty. He heard it in the hallway air, because here, the only sounds came from distant people separated from him by walls. He saw it in the blank beige paint staring back at him. He tasted it and it was flavored like disappointment.

Had he been a fool to hope he could win her

back? His plan was likely a waste of her time and his. Why would telling her the truth about his upcoming assignment and writing her poetry make a difference? He was an airman, exactly what she'd always made clear to him she didn't want. He'd just come back from six months in Syria and in six more months would be restationed to Germany.

She could date any number of guys who lived here and who'd never leave her.

Running his hands through his hair, he told himself to return to his car. But his body refused to obey.

• • •

Have you called Eli? one of Aubrey's friends texted Penelope. *If not, I'll reach out to him. I'm sure he'd be willing to ask Theo's friends to pray.*

Eli! Realization bolted through Penelope, the same type of realization she'd experienced in college once when she'd checked her bedside clock and comprehended that she'd slept through her history exam.

She looked at her watch. 3:46.

Her pacing halted. She'd been treading a route from where Madeline was still sleeping in the master bedroom, to the living area, and back again while she made calls and sent text messages. At first, she'd been focused on trying to reach Theo, who, as it turned out, had been on a business call on his phone. Once she'd finally gotten ahold of him, she'd contacted her parents, Aubrey's mom, and Aubrey's friends. She'd been relaying the story of what had happened and asking everyone to pray.

She'd been so consumed with all of that, she'd totally forgotten about her appointment with Eli.

I'll reach out to Eli now, she replied to Aubrey's friend. Then she dialed Eli's number.

"Hi." He didn't sound annoyed.

"Hi. Listen, I'm terribly sorry." She explained yet again what had happened with Aubrey.

"Don't worry about it." His composed voice lowered her blood pressure better than hypertension pills.

She pulled air to the bottom of her lungs. Let it out slowly.

"What can I do to help?" he asked.

"Would you be willing to contact Theo's other friends and ask them to pray?"

"Of course. Anything else?"

"Not that I can think of right now. I'm believing that she's going to be completely fine."

"I'm believing that, too."

A momentary pause. "Your voice is as warm

and calm as a throw blanket fresh out of the dryer." She came to a stop in the sun next to Madeline's baby swing. "When you fly fighter planes for a living, I'm guessing that nothing rattles you."

"Not true."

"Really?"

"You rattle me."

She let his words drift and spin within her. "You fly missions over Syria, but *I* rattle you?"

"Yes."

"I'm harmless."

"No. All the women I met before you were harmless. You're the opposite of harmless."

Funny, because ever since she'd become acquainted with Eli she'd been convinced that *he* was the dangerous one.

Even after they hung up, the line between her heart and his remained in place, like a golden strand of silk.

● ● ●

Penelope's Vans felt three times as heavy as usual as she climbed the stairs to her apartment that night.

The doctors had determined that Aubrey had no internal bleeding. *Praise the Lord, praise the*

Lord. They'd adjusted her medications in hopes of mitigating the dizziness and the drop in blood pressure she'd experienced. Then they'd sent her home.

Penelope hadn't been able to shake her regret about her lack of vigilance. As soon as Aubrey and Theo returned, she'd blurted out more apologies. Theo and Aubrey had taken her by the shoulders and assured her that they didn't blame her. That she'd done a great job, even.

Still, remorse and fear took a lot out of a person. Penelope was good for absolutely nothing at this point except a quick shower and a freefall onto her mattress.

Her key made its familiar sound as it turned in the lock. On the floor just inside her apartment, the foyer light revealed a folded piece of white paper.

Strange. Had someone pushed this under her door? She scooped it up and opened it.

You are everything.

I think a lot about how

wonderful you are.

—Eli

She lifted a hand to cover her mouth and read it again. Then three more times.

In a bid to win her attention, Roy leapt onto a high shelf of a bookcase, sliding wildly and shoving a few paperbacks off the edge.

"Yes, I see you there," Penelope informed him. "Hang on a second and then I'll bathe you in attention."

Eli had said he wanted to give her something today. This must be what he'd meant. When she'd stood him up, he'd slipped it under her door.

Was this a . . . poem?

The way he'd arranged the words in lines made her think of poetry. Haiku? She remembered from Ms. Mitchell's elementary school class that haiku was five, seven, and five syllables. Right?

She read it again, counting the syllables.

Eli Price had written a haiku poem for her.

Oh . . . *wait.* Understanding lifted like the tip of a rising sun in her mind. The night they'd shared the fried chicken dinner, she'd listed three concerns about dating him. What had she said to him exactly?

She'd said . . . She chewed her lip, remembering. She'd said she worried he couldn't be truthful. He'd told her on the Fourth of July that his squadron was being reassigned in January.

She'd told him she worried he couldn't share his feelings, and he'd written a poem.

He was a goal-oriented person and he was addressing each of her concerns in turn.

What was left? She'd said something about him being so strait-laced that she didn't think he'd be willing to make a fool of himself for love.

Was he going to make a fool of himself next?

She lowered onto her sofa. "Come here, Roy." Her cat sprang from surface to surface, eventually landing on her lap. He gave her a chiding look that clearly said, *Where've you been?*

"Sorry. Family emergency." Distractedly, she rubbed his head while continuing to stare at the poem.

This gesture from Eli was so very, very sweet. She'd been wrapped up in her brother's family's needs for hours. But this paper told her that Eli *saw* her.

That Eli cared.

His thoughtfulness brought tears to her eyes. It seemed like time to revisit her dating rule. It had served her well for a long time. But was it still serving her if it was keeping her from Eli?

Despite the hardships that dating Eli would bring, it could be that he'd be truly, delightfully *good* for her. It could be that a relationship with him would be worth much more than the costs.

• • •

"This team needs to develop the eye of the tiger," Eli informed the Sharpshooters when they gathered just outside the sports complex twenty minutes before Monday night's game. "Does anyone know what that means?"

"Orange?" one kid suggested.

"Is it like the eye of a tornado?" another asked.

"The eye of the tiger," Eli told them, "is about competitiveness. Think about tigers and what their eyes look like when they hunt. They're focused. Intense. They work hard. They're deadly. We're going to have the eye of the tiger tonight. We're going on the hunt, focused and intense. And we're going to try to win one for Coach Theo, because he and his family have been going through a hard time lately. I'm sure he could really use some good news."

"So . . . what's our surprise?" the freckle-faced kid wondered.

Eli pulled a small, round tub out of his gym bag. "Hair gel."

"Hair gel!" They all made faces of disgust. An offended rumble went through the group.

"We're going to take this gel and we're going

112

to make mohawks out of your hair so that you'll look as big, intimidating, and ferocious on the outside as I know you are on the inside."

"The hair of the tiger!" one of them shouted.

"That's right," Eli acknowledged. "Part of winning is having the right attitude and you guys could use a little more swagger. We're going to have the hair of the tiger and the eye of the tiger. And, remember, if you steal the ball or rebound, you also get the claw of the tiger tattooed on your bicep."

"I want mine tattooed on my butt," the class clown stated.

"No, your bicep."

"I want mine on my forehead."

"No, your bicep," Eli insisted. "But before you can get a tattoo at all, you have to . . ." He gave them an expectant look.

"Steal or rebound," several of them said in unison.

"Now form a line to get your mohawk."

"Are you going to have a mohawk too, Coach?"

"Will it fire you guys up if I do?" Eli asked.

"*Yes!*"

"Then bring on the mohawk."

Eli, his hair heavy and sticky, led his battle unit

into the gym. Some of the kids looked great with mohawks. Some looked like porcupines.

When they broke their pre-game huddle they did so with a loud cry of, "For Coach Theo!"

During the game, Eli moved up and down the sideline in front of his bench, shouting instructions, gesturing, sending in subs.

Creighton didn't have time for his phone. He spent the entire game keeping track of steals and rebounds and applying the tiger claw tattoos.

Luckily, the Bricklayers really did throw up bricks. They were just as bad as Eli's team.

When the clock started to count down the game's final minute, both teams had just twelve points each. A Bricklayer released a shot that looked surprisingly decent.

"Don't go in," Eli whispered under his breath. It hit the backboard, bounced off the hoop, seemed to think about its direction for a moment, then dropped harmlessly off the side.

Redhead gave a tiger roar as he thrust himself into the air and managed to come down with the rebound. He passed it to his teammate.

Creighton clapped three times. "Hustle out there, guys. *Hustle!*"

"Go, go, go!" Eli yelled.

Their shortest player ran down the court, a blur

of out-of-control arms and legs. He continued too far under the basket, realized his mistake, dribbled back around and through the mass of bodies that had just arrived. Then he took a shot.

Airball.

Class Clown caught it. "That counts as a rebound!" he yelled at Eli.

"Shoot!" Eli urged him.

He threw the ball up. It went very high and then dropped a long way—right through the net with a *swish*.

The entire team erupted into howls of joy. So much so, they almost forgot to activate the full court press when the other team tried to rush toward their own basket. The Sharpshooters found their places just in time. Guarded with all their hearts.

The buzzer sounded. Eli punched a fist into the air. "Yes!"

The boys reacted as if they'd just won the NBA Championship Trophy, crowding into each other in an excited, jumping mass. Eli joined them, whooping and grinning.

The old saying *If at first you don't succeed, try, try, try again* slid through his mind.

He hadn't succeeded yet with Penelope.

But if there was hope for the Sharpshooters, there had to be hope for him, too.

Chapter Nine

On Tuesday afternoon, Penelope spotted Jodi walking toward Polka-Dot Apron Pies. Before the older woman could so much as offer a greeting, Penelope leaned onto her wrists and jutted as far as possible out the trailer's order window. "Interested in an even exchange?"

Jodi tucked a strand of long brown hair behind her ear and lifted a pleasant expression toward Penelope. "What kind of exchange?"

"Your advice for my pie."

"I'm happy to give you advice for free."

"And I'm happy to give you pie for free in return."

Jodi's oldest son practiced soccer near here on Tuesday afternoons, and Jodi often swung by with her two younger kids after dropping him off. Penelope knew the pie preferences of every member of Jodi's family of five. She waved a hand toward Jodi's thirteen-year-old girl and ten-year-old boy. "Are you three in the mood for Theo's Pie, Theo's Pie, and mixed berry?"

"Yes, please."

"Grab a table and I'll meet you there."

While Kevin plated, she went through her leave-work routine. Take off polka-dot apron. Release hair from topknot. Grab purse.

"Done for the day?" Kevin asked her.

"Yep."

He passed her the three slices, then held the door for her. "See ya, boss."

"See ya later, Kevin."

"It's been a good one."

"It has!"

He raised a hand in a parting wave. "I really appreciate working here."

"I'm glad."

He blushed with pleasure.

She edged away.

In classic Kevin fashion, he didn't turn back into the trailer. Mr. Never-Know-When-To-End-An-Exchange lingered.

"Kevin?"

"Mm?"

"You're dismissed," she told him, like a kindly teacher to a student.

"Yes, ma'am." He gave a salute that looked

nothing like a soldier's salute and, beaming, finally closed the door behind her.

Penelope joined Jodi at one of the round, white metal tables lining the sidewalk in front of Misty River's three food trucks. Jodi encouraged her kids to take their pie to a spot on the grass. Agreeably, they moved off and out of earshot.

"What type of advice are you in need of?" Jodi asked.

"Dating advice."

Jodi's rectangular face brightened. "Tell all."

Penelope explained her dating rule, the reasons why she'd stuck to it all these years, and why Eli Price was making her ponder the merits of riddling her rule with buckshot.

Jodi dabbed her mouth with a napkin and sat back, giving Penelope a fond smile. "I sometimes think that when God hears us making statements about our future plans, what we *will* and *will not* do, He laughs. Then He rubs his hands together and says, 'We'll see about that.'"

"Gah."

"There's a verse . . . I wish I could remember it exactly. But, to paraphrase, it basically says that we can make plans, but it's the Lord who will determine our steps."

"I've lived by my rule for ten years."

"And I totally get why you made that rule for yourself. But if God has other ideas or it's no longer what you want for yourself, you have the power to unmake your rule. There's no shame in that. It's not that you failed at rule-keeping. It's just that circumstances changed."

Penelope explained that, since receiving Eli's haiku, she'd texted him her thanks. He'd said *you're welcome.* And that had been it. "You've been married to a fighter pilot for a while," Penelope said. "Should I decide to date Eli, what pros and what cons should I expect?"

"Based on what you've told me, you already have a good grip on the cons. The girlfriends, boyfriends, wives, and husbands of those in the military don't have it easy. At all. Long absences are rough on relationships." She followed the progress of her spork as she swirled it through mixed berries. "It was particularly rough on me when our kids were small. I'd function as a single mom for months at a time. Then when Chris came home, I'd need to immediately adjust back to being a married mom with a husband at home."

"I can imagine."

"You'll come into contact with plenty of people who'll disapprove of the politics of whatever president's in office. They'll give you an earful about all the ways the president is mishandling the military."

Penelope winced. She loathed politics.

"Should you date someone in the military, you'll have to accept that their duty will often come before you. Sometimes they'll be given a choice and they'll have to try to balance what's best for their relationship with what's best for their career. Other times, they won't be given a choice."

"I understand."

Jodi swallowed a bite. Her focus meandered to her kids. They'd finished their pie and were now sitting cross-legged facing each other. The older sister was teaching her brother a hand-clap routine.

Jodi's gaze returned to Penelope. "Loving someone in the military requires great sacrifice. But it also comes with great reward." Her eyes harbored years of experience, her mouth a curl of tenderness. "I married a hero, Penelope. I've never lost sight of that."

Penelope nodded.

"The men and women who do this work are courageous. What could be a greater honor than loving and supporting someone who's given their oath to protect their country and their countrymen, even at the cost of their own life?"

"I can't think of one," Penelope answered, humbled. Put that way, her pie-making contribution to the world seemed very small.

"I'm incredibly proud of Chris."

Penelope thought of Eli, in Syria for months. Flying mission after mission there. Dealing with the discomforts and the pressures. Executing his job. Committed.

"Another positive," Jodi continued, "is that I've made friends who've become closer to me than family members. This life fosters amazingly deep friendships. My friends have had my back so many times."

A few minutes passed while Jodi finished her pie.

"What are you going to do?" Jodi asked.

Penelope groaned. "I can't believe I'm saying this, but after all this time, I'm leaning toward dissolving my ironclad dating rule. It's just . . . it's just that I'm concerned. He's leaving in six months. Is your family going to Germany, too?"

"We are."

"Do you think it's smart for me to start something with Eli now?"

Jodi lifted a shoulder. "A lot can happen in six months. I'd suggest you do what your heart tells you to do, then let God determine your steps."

• • •

Around dinnertime the following night, Penelope was absorbed in an episode of *The Great British Baking Show* when a knock sounded on her door.

She startled and Roy pounced straight up into the air. He landed furtively. His flat face asked, *Expecting anyone?*

"Nope." She rose, the farfetched hope that it might be Eli tugging upward inside her like a kite. She aligned her eye with the door's peephole.

Not Eli. Aubrey and Theo, who held Madeline in her baby carrier over one of his arms, stood in the hallway. The kite swooped back to earth.

Penelope ushered them inside, exclaiming over how great they all looked. Aubrey, in a sundress with her hair flat-ironed. Theo, in a white business shirt open at the neck. They'd dressed Madeline in an outfit Penelope had given her—a one-piece with cherries on it and a matching red headband.

"This is almost more baby cuteness than I can stand, you realize," Penelope told them. "Hello, darling itty-bitty human. Your preciousness meter broke because it couldn't keep up."

Madeline sucked her pacifier, looking content to be in the care of both her parents instead of the care of her well-meaning but inexperienced aunt.

Penelope waved them to seats in the living area.

"I haven't left the house in days and I was desperate for a change of scenery," Aubrey said.

"We're on our way out for dinner," Theo said.

"Okay, but you're going to take things very easy, right?" Penelope couldn't help but ask her sister-in-law. After Sunday's events, she didn't trust Aubrey not to slump over, unconscious, at any moment.

"Very easy. The most strenuous thing I've done today is walk up that flight of stairs." Aubrey hooked a thumb toward the building's staircase.

Penelope regarded her with concern.

"Penelope, Aubrey's going to be fine," Theo said. "The clot is gone, and they think they have her medicines calibrated just right. Her medical team is on top of things. It's very unlikely that she'll have a relapse."

"Yes! Of course. I know."

"Really? Because ever since Sunday you've seemed a little traumatized," Theo told her.

"Which I totally understand," Aubrey said. "It must have been an awful shock to find me passed out like that."

"I'm just glad you're all right. I'm sorry again that I wasn't with you when it happened—"

"Look into my face," Theo said to her sternly. He leaned forward, planting his elbows on his knees. "You don't have to apologize to us again. You were there that day because *you* were doing *us* a favor."

Aubrey regarded her with sweet sincerity. "Even if you'd been right beside me, I would have fainted."

"Yes, but if I'd been beside you, I could have intervened to help you sooner."

"How could you have done more than you did?" Theo asked. "She came to when her body was ready to come to."

"You've done so many favors for us this past week and a half," Aubrey said. "You've gone above and beyond."

"No—"

"Yes," Theo insisted. "Thanks for everything."

Love for them washed over Penelope like a waterfall shower. "You're welcome."

She'd learned that taking care of a newborn was hard. Physically hard. But the mental weight of the responsibility was hard to bear, too. Aubrey's medical issues: also hard.

The three people in front of her were a living reminder that love isn't always rosy. Love demands effort. Sometimes it's scary. The hardships that come with love will refine you with painful fire. But if you let them, the difficulties can also deepen love.

Madeline's pacifier went *squeak squeak squeak*.

Roy zeroed in on the pacifier the way he would a hummingbird. "Roy." Penelope activated his soft, flopping fish toy, then tossed it. The cat skidded across the room to it, batted it. Skidded. Gnawed on it. Rolled on his back, clasping it in his paws.

"Go get ready," Theo said to Penelope. "You're coming with us to dinner."

"I am?"

"Yes," he answered. "And we're leaving in ten minutes because I've been starving for the last half hour. Another half hour from now I'll be seriously cranky."

She hurried to the bathroom and freshened her makeup. While brushing her teeth, she contemplated her clothing options. She settled on a dove gray V-neck T-shirt, black jeans ripped at both knees, and the pair of shoes she wore only when feeling adventurous. Leopard-print Vans.

• • •

They ate at Whiskey's because it was Aubrey's favorite. With its wooden chandeliers, art-covered walls, and servers wearing red plaid ties, Whiskey's environment served "upscale pub" almost as effectively as the fare.

Wednesday nights were karaoke night at Whiskey's, and a fifty-something woman was currently singing the obligatory karaoke song "I Will Survive" from the small stage located next to the front windows.

Penelope relished the flavors of her steak salad and admired how comfortable her brother looked, holding his baby in the crook of his arm and giving her a bottle.

The karaoke microphone gave a squawk followed by a gap of quiet.

She leaned toward Aubrey. "What are your plans for—"

The opening bars of a familiar, old-timey song coasted across the restaurant.

"'You never close your eyes anymore when I kiss your lips,'" a male voice sang. A *recognizable* male voice.

Surprise shot a tingle down Penelope's spine. She forgot the question she'd been about to ask Aubrey and twisted in her seat.

Eli stood on the stage in front of the microphone, grinning.

Penelope's eyes went wide and an astonished huff of amusement escaped.

He was performing the song she'd cajoled him into singing on prior occasions. But those times, they'd been surrounded by a small number of their friends. This time, a large number of strangers were watching. The restaurant was packed.

Light gleamed against his brown-blond hair and the shoulders of his navy henley. He looked tall and built in his jeans and battered leather lace-up boots.

Eli was a mediocre-to-bad singer. God had blessed him with so many abilities. Vocal talent, too, would not have been fair.

All at once, four of Eli's friends, including Sam, crowded onto the stage behind him and joined in for the chorus. "'You've lost that lovin' feelin'.'"

Penelope's cheeks creased with amusement. How in the world had Eli convinced guarded Sam to step in as his backup singer?

She stole a glance at Theo. He gave her a jaunty eyebrow lift and wink. Ah. This was a setup. Eli must have contacted Theo, spilled the beans about his courtship plans, and enlisted Theo's help.

It seemed that their table wasn't the only table that'd taken notice of the performers. All the women in the place had swiveled toward the front. This was the best entertainment to hit Misty River, perhaps ever.

"Woo-hoo!" a grandmother called.

"Yes!" A curly-haired blonde danced in her seat, arms overhead. "I'll give you that loving feeling!"

"Now there's no welcome hook in the skies when I preach to you," Eli sang. He'd messed up the lyrics of that line because he was watching her and paying too little attention to the words on the screen.

She burst out laughing.

"And now you're um um um butterflies little wings I flew."

More laughter welled up in her.

His backup singers joined in on each chorus, winning everyone over with their enthusiasm. The diners surrounding her began clapping in time. When they reached the final "Bring back that lovin' feelin'" refrain, everyone in the place sang along.

Eli's performance was simultaneously sexy and adorable. She *could not believe* he'd done this . . . for her.

Uproarious applause shook the room when they finished.

Someone shouted, "More! More!" And numerous voices took up the chant.

Eli attempted to pass the microphone to Sam,

but Sam backed away, making a *no way* signal with his hands.

One of Eli's other buddies took up the gauntlet and began singing "Don't Stop Believin'."

Eli stepped off the stage and stood near the door, his vision trained on her with affection, uncertainty, humor. *Did you like it?* he mouthed.

She rushed to her feet and wove through the tables. When she reached him, she grabbed his hand and pulled him outside. Mellow, peachy light flowed over them.

She towed him around the edge of Whiskey's, then behind to a secluded spot near a tree. They faced each other, her hand still in his.

"You made a fool of yourself for me," she said.

"Yeah. If you want me to make an even bigger fool of myself, I can always go back in and massacre Whitney Houston's 'I Will Always Love You.'"

"That won't be necessary."

"No?"

"No. You made an adequate fool of yourself and allayed the last of my worries about you. I loved the song. Thank you."

"You're welcome." His handsome face settled into serious lines. "I'm crazy about you."

Instinctively, she placed her free hand over her

heart, to seal in the power of his words. "I'm crazy about you, too."

His eyes glowed with the intensity of his hope.

She was about to risk a lot. To put herself out there, trust him, and, in doing so, open herself up to potential future sorrow. But she had a feeling he—*they*—might be worth the risk.

Sometimes, in order to grab hold of something good, you had to empty your hands. And so, very purposely, she let go of the concerns she'd been clutching that had separated her from Eli. She was going to have to trust God to work out their future.

The only choice she had before her today: yes or no to giving Eli a chance.

"I . . ." She bit her lower lip. Released it. "I hereby issue an amendment to my dating rule."

A slow, lopsided smile moved across his lips.

"My rule still stands except in the case of one particular airman. Eli Price is exempt from my rule. Effective immediately." She reached up, her fingers tunneling into the hair at the back of his neck, delighting in the feel of it.

His hands slid up to cup her jaw. "Penelope?"

"Yes?"

"That's really, really good news."

She could feel his heat, sense his goodness, see

his devotion in the carved angles of his face.

"I feel like that character from *Green Eggs and Ham*," she whispered.

"The Dr. Seuss book?"

"Exactly! One of the characters kept trying to get the other to try green eggs and ham. But the other character wouldn't. Until right at the end—"

He kissed her.

It was a kiss for the record books, gilded and glittering, full of rightness and feelings deep and true and demanding.

After what could have been five minutes or fifty—she'd lost track of concepts as unimportant as time—he pulled back an inch.

Their shallow breaths intermingled. "Do you like green eggs and ham?" he whispered.

"So very, *very* much," she said, pressing her lips back to his.

"We can make our plans,
but the Lord determines our steps."
Proverbs 16:9 NLT

Fall in love with Sam Turner within the pages of *Stay with Me*, the first full-length novel in the MISTY RIVER ROMANCE series by Becky Wade.

Stay with Me

Loving her is a risk he can't afford ... and can't resist.

When acclaimed Bible study author Genevieve Woodward receives an anonymous letter referencing her parents' past, she returns to her hometown in the Blue Ridge mountains to case down her family's secret. However, it's Genevieve's own secret that catches up to her when Sam Turner, owner of an historic farm, uncovers the source of shame she's worked so hard to hide.

Sam has embraced his sorrow, his isolation, and his identity as an outsider. He's spent years carving out both career success and peace of mind. The last thing he wants is to rent the cottage on his property to a woman whose struggles stir his worst failure back to life. Yet, can he bear to turn her away when she needs him most?

Romances by Becky Wade

MISTY RIVER ROMANCE
Take a Chance on Me (#0.5)
Stay with Me (#1)

BRADFORD SISTERS ROMANCE
Then Came You (#0.5)
True to You (#1)
Falling for You (#2)
Because of You (#2.5)
Sweet on You (#3)

THE PORTER FAMILY
Undeniably Yours (#1)
Meant to Be Mine (#2)
A Love Like Ours (#3)
The Proposal (#3.5)
Her One and Only (#4)

Stand-alone Romances
My Stubborn Heart
Love in the Details

Sign up for Becky's E-Newsletter

For the latest news about Becky's upcoming books, exclusive giveaways, and more subscribe to Becky's free quarterly e-newsletter at www.beckywade.com

About the Author

Becky Wade's a California native who attended Baylor University, met and married a Texan, and settled in Dallas. She published historical romances for the general market before putting her career on hold for several years to care for her three children. When God called her back to writing, Becky knew He meant for her to turn her attention to Christian fiction. She loves writing funny, modern, and inspirational contemporary romance! She's the Christy and Carol Award–winning author of *My Stubborn Heart*, the PORTER FAMILY series, and the BRADFORD SISTERS ROMANCE series. To learn more about Becky and her books, visit her website at beckywade.com.

Connect with Becky

You'll find Becky on Facebook as Author Becky Wade and on Twitter, Instagram, and Pinterest as BeckyWadeWriter.

Made in the USA
Monee, IL
04 November 2021